Hitched

Volume 1

Kendall Ryan

Hitched, Volume One

Developmental Editing by Alexandra Fresch

Copy Editing by Pam Berehulke

Cover design by Hang Le

This book is a work of fiction. Names, characters, places, and incidents are either the product of the author's imagination or are used fictitiously.

Praise for Hitched

"I'm literally in love with HITCHED The irreverent humor, fun storyline and intriguing characters enchanted me immediately and I was hooked. I mean really, when a book has a chapter with only the two words being "Game on" (right after the chapter where Noah pulls his big boy parts out in a swanky bar) you know this is going to be a fun and funny read! And Ms. Ryan didn't disappoint...she kept me cracking up the entire read! I'm salivating for the next installment!"

—The Romance Reviews

"Fun, flirty and steamy, Hitched will have you addicted from the first word! Kendall Ryan delivered big time, I'm practically salivating for more!"

—Angie and Jessica's Dreamy Reads

"Kendall Ryan strikes gold in her latest super star, Hitched, a romantic comedy spiked with steam, anchored by angst, and flooded with feelings."

—Bookalicious Babes Blog

"Charming, swoony and playful, Kendall Ryan's Hitched left me salivating for more. More Noah, more Olivia, more of this series which already has my heart all aflutter, my smile perma-pinned to my face, and my mind aching for answers."

—Give Me Books

"Hitched was a perfect non-stop read! I read it in one sitting, and laughed so many times my belly ached. It's a fun, romantic read with a light-hearted story that made me ache for more when I finished."

About the Book

Marry the girl I've had a crush on my whole life? Check.

Inherit a hundred-billion-dollar company? Check.

Produce an heir... Wait, what?

I have ninety days to knock up my brand-new fake wife. There's only one problem—she hates my guts.

And in the fine print of the contract? The requirement that we produce an heir.

She can't stand to be in the same room with me. Says she'll never be in my bed. But I've never backed down from a challenge and I'm not about to start now.

Mark my words—I'll have her begging for me, and it won't take ninety days.

Prologue

Noah

"Another beer?" my best friend Sterling asks.

"I better not."

He smirks. "So you're really going to go through with it, huh, mate?"

"What's the big deal? You took a fake date to prom."

I chuckle to myself, remembering the year Sterling took his cousin to the dance. He thought it was genius at the time—no corsage to buy, no need to impress her with a fancy restaurant or limo ride. Until the end of the night, when all the rest of us were enjoying some skin-to-skin contact with our dates, and he realized what a horrible decision he'd made. The only skin-to-skin action he got was with his hand.

"A fake wife is a hell of a lot different. It's a big fucking deal." Sterling glares at me over the rim of his beer.

Looking out over the ocean from our spot on the porch of the beach cottage, I loosen my tie, which has grown too tight around my neck, and level him with a dark stare.

"Actually, it's legally binding, so she'll be my real wife. Until we got divorced, or got the marriage annulled or whatever."

"Do you even hear yourself? This is insane. You can't marry some chick you don't even like."

"Who says I don't like her?"

His eyes widen. "I'm not talking about the unrequited lust-fueled crush you've had on her since you were a horny teenager."

I rub the back of my neck, feeling the stirrings of a headache. "What do you expect me to do? It's part of my father's will. This is my—no, *our* condition for taking over the company. No marriage means no inheritance, period. For either of us."

Some people may say that being thrust into such

luxury from the start makes you immune to it all, but that's not true. I've never taken a single day of it for granted, and there's no way in hell I'm going to give it up without a fight.

Sterling releases a loud sigh, and his gaze follows mine out to the water beyond. "I just think you should really think this through, man. Marriage is a big deal. It's not something to be entered into lightly."

Between the two of us, Sterling's always been the voice of reason. For every brazen and rash idea I've had, every time I've jumped into the deep end without thinking, he's helped steer me back onto the straight-and-narrow path. He's been my best friend since we were fourteen. As the two new kids at a prestigious boarding school in Connecticut, we became inseparable.

"Trust me when I tell you I understand the gravity of the situation."

My father's death last year was a huge wake-up call. The fate of his $100 billion company suddenly dropped straight into my hands. I had to be ready to take over. And I am—I'll do whatever it takes. Of course, it doesn't hurt that my bride-to-be is the woman I've always wanted.

"There has to be another way," Sterling says after taking a sip of his beer. "Besides, with your wandering eye and perpetually hard dick, you'd make a terrible husband."

Ouch. I'm not that bad, am I?

He's lecturing me about something, but all I can focus on is the tumultuous waves and the uneasy feelings stirring inside me.

"Oh, one more thing," I say, turning toward him. "I need to knock her up."

Sterling spits out his drink.

Chapter One

Noah

One Month Earlier...

I clench my teeth and check my Rolex for the third time. This entire thing is a huge waste of time.

"Where is she?" I cast a glance at Olivia's father, Fred Cane, who's seated at the head of the long conference room table.

"She'll be here," he assures me. Then, under his breath, he adds, "She's got to."

My sentiments exactly.

This meeting is a last-ditch effort to try to convince Olivia to sign the contract. But I'm worried today will just be a repeat of last week. She flat-out refused to sign anything that put the two of us together in the same sentence—and said *hell no.*

Actually, it might have been said with more gusto. I

think there was even an f-bomb involved.

But we need to get hitched before ownership of Tate & Cane Enterprises can transfer to us. And with the board of directors' deadline looming, we need to do it yesterday. I'm not losing the $100 billion company that my father built because the ice queen won't play nice.

I make a fat six-figure income, enjoy the finest indulgences money can buy, and I know damn well I live the good life. Just because I don't take it for granted doesn't mean I don't take advantage.

Free upgrades at all the best hotels? *Absolutely*. The finest champagne delivered to my table, courtesy of the sommelier? *Why not?* The lifeguard at our country club letting me bend her over in the locker room all summer? *Sure*. The pretty blond hostess at La Chample who wants to blow me in the bathroom before my business dinner? *Hell yeah*. Being wealthy and attractive has its perks.

But if Olivia doesn't show up today, and if we can't agree on the terms of this contract, my wealth stands to suffer immensely. As do the jobs and lives of the six thousand employees of Tate & Cane, including one of my favorite people on the planet, Rosita Hernandez. She's a single mom to six kids. And if this deal goes south, I can only imagine what would happen to someone like Rosita. Christ, I'd probably end up moving her and the kids into my penthouse. Which would obviously put a huge cramp in the aforementioned blow jobs and champagne I regularly enjoy.

I shudder at the thought.

"I know it's unconventional, that the contract is . . ." Fred pauses and frowns. He drums his fingers on the table, looking sheepish.

Unconventional? To say the fucking least. If the situation weren't so grim, I might laugh.

He and my father drew up their wills years ago, outlining what would happen to their multibillion-dollar baby should they kick the bucket. The daunting stack of papers in front of me spells out in full legal jargon that Olivia and I are to inherit the company with joint fifty-fifty ownership . . . but only if we're legally wed.

With Fred's failing health and the company itself suffering six consecutive quarters in the red, an emergency meeting was called last week. Olivia and I were presented with our options.

In my view, there were no options. There was just the right thing to do. We had to marry to save not only our own jobs, but our fathers' legacies and the jobs of six thousand people in offices in Manhattan, Chicago, San Diego, and Brussels.

Olivia felt differently. She didn't relish the idea of being tied to me, and insisted there had to be another way.

Even if we do manage to persuade her to tie the knot, there's no way Olivia would be getting anywhere near my bed. *Damn shame.*

We came close once . . . just once. Back when she was a drunk college co-ed on spring break.

Her family was staying with mine in a beach house on Puget Sound. We'd escaped the East Coast for the West that summer. Whale watching and hiking trips in the salty sea air and evenings spent eating lobster and drinking chardonnay like we were real adults and not nineteen-year-olds with stars in our eyes.

She snuck out of the bunk bed in the room she was sharing with her sister, Rachel, and into my bedroom that night. And when she crawled in beside me and laid her warm palm against my bare chest, I was a goner. I've always wanted Olivia. Always desired her, from before I even knew what those strange feelings were in my gut, my chest. We kissed in the darkness, our tongues exploring, hands groping, hearts beating wildly.

But then reality slammed into me. There were a lot of reasons I told her no that night. Her mom had recently been diagnosed with cancer, and I knew Olivia would regret using me to cope. Plus, I knew from a recent game of Truth or Dare that she was still a virgin.

So I kissed her a final time and then sent her away. It was the hardest thing I've ever done.

And now she treats me as if I were a piece of gum stuck to the bottom of those Louboutin heels she favors.

"I really think this is for the best," Fred adds,

pulling me back to the present.

"It's what your father wanted, Noah," Prescott says. Before my father's death, Prescott was his most trusted advisor. He's also a total fucking douche bag.

Just then, the conference room door flies open, and I know it's her before I even look up from the contract.

A fresh floral scent with crisp notes of honeysuckle greets me. I have no idea where Olivia gets that shit, but it makes my mouth water. It always has. I once spent an entire Saturday at the fragrance counter of a department store trying to figure it out, trying to prove that it was just some manufactured, bottled version of attraction, that it wasn't something special to her. I never found it.

"I'm here," Olivia says, slightly breathless.

I look up just in time to be treated to the sight of her smoothing her dress shirt over her curves. Lush breasts and a flat stomach leading to full hips. Her jacket is slung over her arm, as is her tan leather briefcase, monogrammed with her initials in black cursive stitching.

"Miss Cane," I say cheerfully. "You look exceptionally refreshed this morning."

She likes to exercise in the morning before work, says it gives her the mental agility to stay focused on business for the sixteen-hour days she's known to plow through. I like that it gives her cheeks a rosy glow . . . much like I'd guess sex would. Just the thought makes my cock twitch in my dress slacks.

"Save it, Noah. This is purely business," she says, blinking at me with those lush, dark lashes.

No smile. No laughter. The opposite of the usual reaction I evoke from the fairer sex. And that annoys the shit out of me.

It's as if Olivia Cane alone possesses an antidote to my charm. And that only makes me want to watch her surrender to me that much more. The idea of her on her knees, pink lips parted, taking my cock deep down her throat, begging for more even as she gags on my impressive length, is more than just a sexual turn-on. It's practically a life goal. To me, sex is a competitive sport. I know the rules, I play hard, and I always win.

Realizing they're all still watching me, I take a deep breath, trying to force my cock to behave himself, and hold up my hands. She's never taken one ounce of my shit, and I respect the hell out of her for that.

"I'm just trying to do what's best here."

She lets out a soft sigh of exasperation and sets her bag on the table. "Let's get on with this."

Her father pats the back of her hand. "Sit down, honey."

She obeys, poised even in defeat, lowering herself into the seat with the confidence that was bred into her from birth. Preston slides a copy of the contract over to her, and she leafs through it with disinterest.

"I just don't see why there has to be a marriage clause in the will."

The woman has a point. My guess? Because our fathers have always wanted to play matchmaker when it came to us. They've paired us together since we were in diapers. Hell, we even have an old photo of us in full wedding apparel at a fake wedding from some twenty years ago.

"I've explained this, darling. It's the only way we keep the company in the family. I thought that's what you wanted . . . a chance to run this place someday."

"I do, Dad," she says softly. Then her eyes lift to mine. "I just didn't think I'd be forced into something like this."

"No one's forcing you," I say, keeping my tone light as I lace my fingers behind my head. "The choice is yours, Olivia. I already told you, I'm game."

She chews on her red lacquered thumbnail for just a second before folding her hands in her lap and shooting me an icy glare. "I'm quite aware of your position."

Hell, at least she's willing to hear us all out again. I know that deep down, she understands our fathers' rationale. We're stronger together. Our families built this company together. Neither of us can afford to buy the other out, so it needs to stay jointly fifty-fifty within the family. For now.

But for me, it's about more than just money. Olivia and I grew up together; our parents always envisioned us ending up together. I always knew she'd be somewhere in my future, even if it was just working side by side, with her busting my balls every chance she got. It was something I looked forward to.

Fred continued. "Trust and loyalty are the most important things in business. We can't go getting into bed with someone we don't know. We have to keep all of this in this room. Just between family."

Olivia sighs, giving him a skeptical look. "I'll think about it."

At least it wasn't a flat *no* this time, even if her tone is still sour.

Prescott lets out an annoyed huff. "We'll meet again on Thursday."

She stuffs the contract in her bag and rises from the table, seemingly in a hurry to escape. "Until then."

"Thank you for keeping an open mind," her father says. "These things have a way of working themselves out in ways you can't anticipate."

I accept Fred and Prescott's good-bye handshakes.

When Olivia's turn comes, she thrusts her hand at me, clearly wanting to just get this over with . . . and I have a flash of wicked inspiration. Maybe I should shake things up. Test how thick her icy shell really is.

Holding her gaze, I raise her hand to my mouth and kiss it. "A pleasure doing business with you . . . Mrs. Tate," I tease in a husky voice, letting my lips graze her knuckles.

Her eyes widen and she sucks in her breath. Is it my imagination, or do her cheeks look a little pinker than before? But before I can be sure, her expression hardens into a death glare.

Snatching back her hand, she snaps, "Don't get ahead of yourself. I haven't agreed to marry you yet, and even if I do, I'm *never* taking your last name."

And then she's gone, leaving me standing there with a stupid grin on my face.

"I've seen that look before," Fred says with a small smile. "You're in trouble, son."

I laugh off his warning. There's no way Olivia Cane will ever have me wrapped around her finger.

Yet her unique sweetness lingers in my nostrils. She must have dabbed that intoxicating scent on her wrist, so close to my nose when I kissed her hand. I can still feel her soft, smooth skin on my lips. Such a small intimacy—just brushing her as I spoke—shouldn't have spread this tingle over me. But there's no denying that this room has become a few degrees too warm.

This is going to be interesting. Hell, it may even be *fun*.

Chapter Two

Olivia

Camryn almost spills her pear mojito and gasps. "You have to do what? With who?"

Nodding grimly, I take a fortifying gulp of sangria. Just explaining this whole harrowing situation makes me feel like I'm going crazy.

We're eating lunch at a table for two at Banderilla, our favorite tapas bar in all of Manhattan. This restaurant has been our go-to hangout spot since we were college roommates.

We've talked over countless decisions here. Whether I should break up with my shitty first boyfriend (I did), whether Camryn should give her anal virginity to her wannabe musician boyfriend (she did), if we should get matching friendship tattoos (I chickened out), whether she should accept Tate & Cane's job offer after the internship I hooked her up with (she did).

But this decision is probably the biggest of my life.

I need my best friend's coolheaded advice now more than ever.

Camryn heaves a sympathetic sigh. "Jesus. I knew the company wasn't doing so hot, but I had no idea just how much trouble we were in."

"Yeah, turns out we should have invested more in social media."

Like all the other big marketing firms. Dad had stuck to his guns with old strategies, and now clients thought we were a dinosaur.

"So, what do you think I should do about this contract?" I ask her again. I try not to sound impatient, but my head has been spinning ever since Dad announced his retirement—and I learned exactly what I'd need to do to take his place.

"Let me make sure I understand. You need to inherit and unfuck T&C, or else the board will pawn it off. Before the next financial quarter."

"Yep."

"But Bill Tate's will says you can't inherit until you

marry his son."

"Uh-huh."

She sucks her teeth. "So . . . down the aisle in a matter of days, huh? Sounds like the board is the rock and Tate's will is the hard place."

"Exactly." Although it's Noah's hard place that I really need to worry about right now. "And between the two, my personal life's about to get smashed into dust."

"I didn't know you had a personal life." She holds up one hand at my exasperated glare. "I'm kidding, I'm kidding. Sorry."

"No, you're right. I don't really." I sigh heavily. "But damn it, why should I give up what little I have? It's not fair. At the end of a long workday, I want to come home to my own space for some peace and quiet."

Not to mention wine. And ice cream. And drowning out the silence with crappy TV so I can't start thinking about how lonely I am.

"I couldn't stand having that jerk in my face 24–7.

I'd put up with him all day at work, and then I'd have to see his dirty socks everywhere." *Fuck no.*

"Who says you have to share your space?"

I snort as I lift a forkful of *papas bravas* to my mouth. "A husband and wife who don't live together? Yeah, that'd look just great for publicity." One of many reasons why Dad would never let me hear the end of it.

Camryn shrugs, her palms turned up. "My point is, you don't necessarily have to lose your whole life."

"Just the parts with independence and privacy."

"Come on, try to think about the situation like any other business move. This marriage is just a piece of paper. After you and Noah deal with the big picture, you can negotiate the details like adults and find something you can both live with. You two are on the same page here—making a huge personal sacrifice to save your company."

"I'm not so sure about that. Noah seems way more into the idea than me. He was on board from the very beginning."

I rub my hand where he kissed it, thinking about the husky way he murmured *Mrs. Tate*. His idea of matrimony clearly isn't very holy.

Camryn raises one perfectly waxed eyebrow. "Oh? You think he likes the idea of sharing a bed with you?"

"I think he likes sharing a bed with anything that has a pulse."

Although his playboy ways make it seem even odder that he's so eager to tie himself down. *Uh, that was a poor choice of words.* But who's to say he won't just keep sleeping around?

Like Camryn said, this marriage is strictly business. A mere legal formality. And Noah would probably explode if he went more than a week without pussy.

I may be the boss's daughter, but I still overhear my fair share of office gossip. Noah nailed all six interns last summer. He's also slept with various secretaries over the years, and everyone just turned a blind eye. Boys will be boys . . .

Well, playtime is over. If he expects to turn this company around, we've got our work cut out for us.

"But how do *you* feel about all this? Noah Tate is pretty fucking hot."

"Camryn . . ." I groan.

"What? I have working eyeballs. His hotness is an objective fact. Just like the pope being Catholic and carbs making you fat. He just is. Would it really be so bad to see him naked?" Her sly smile says she's suggesting a lot more than just *looking*. "As long as we're weighing the pros and cons here . . ."

I pause to consider the image, then grudgingly admit, "No."

In fact, it would probably be pretty damn fantastic. I've already gotten a preview of his toned body, firm chest, and six-pack abs. Whenever our families summered together in the Hamptons, he took every opportunity to strut around shirtless. Hell, when I was nineteen, I came close to fucking him. But I was young and stupid and horny back then. Now I'm older, wiser . . . and still incredibly horny. *Damn it.*

It's ridiculous how easily Noah grabs my attention. The smallest thing he does can leave me flustered. Like at the close of our business meeting yesterday. Just as a bare-bones courtesy, the most brusque good-bye possible, I stuck out my hand at him—only for Noah to bow slightly and raise it to his mouth for a lingering kiss.

"A pleasure doing business with you ... Mrs. Tate," he teased in a husky voice.

My mouth went dry and my stomach fluttered. Or maybe that flutter was somewhere a bit south of my stomach. I suddenly remembered exactly how many years, months, days, and hours it had been since I'd last gotten laid.

I tried to recover. Who the hell did he think he was? We were standing in a Madison Avenue skyscraper, not a sixteenth-century castle. This was wildly inappropriate workplace behavior. I could slap his tight ass with a harassment suit if I wanted. Instead, I just gave the cocky bastard a death glare and the iciest retort I could think of.

But it was too late. There was no denying my body's reaction. The red-hot shiver that had run down my spine when his soft, full lips touched my knuckles, brushing my skin as he spoke.

Even now, I find myself replaying the image of Noah Tate gazing up at me with a sinful smirk, his dark eyes alight . . .

I shake away the steamy memory. So what if Noah knows how to flirt like the shameless manwhore he is? Schmoozing is all he's good for. And handsome men are a dime a dozen, especially in New York. Hell, a fifty-dollar vibrator could do his job, and I wouldn't have to listen to its bullshit. I didn't bust my ass in business school just to become Noah's little woman.

Then again, I also didn't bust my ass in business school to watch my father's company go down the drain, either.

My thoughts sober me, cooling my anger into melancholy. I spent my childhood in my father's office, playing at his feet while he steered a financial ship of thousands. All children think of their parents as gods, and I was no exception. Even since I took my place at his right hand, with my own voice in the family business, I still respect him more than any other man.

And then the cancer diagnosis. Diagnoses, plural—first Mom in my freshman year of college, then Dad just last year.

But even though I'd had a front-row seat to Mom's mortality, Dad's still came as a shock. He's as wise and proud as ever, and he puts up a brave front for the rest of us, but I can tell what the cancer is doing to him. I've been his daughter for twenty-six years; I know where to look. It's those little moments, like when his hands shake when we talk about the future, or he gets that faraway look in his eyes.

Dad has so little time. Sometimes it's still hard to remember that. All too soon, Rachel and I will be each other's only remaining family. And my little sister sure as hell won't run Tate & Cane Enterprises. She has never been interested in the business world; she loves fashion, not finance. Although maybe I should ask her advice on graphic design, for revamping our marketing campaign styles . . .

I frown into my sangria. Damn, I'm thinking as if Tate & Cane is already mine. As if I've subconsciously taken my responsibilities for granted.

Well, why shouldn't I? Dad always told me that his seat would be mine someday. This company is my birthright. It's Dad's legacy—the hard-won fruit of all his blood, sweat, and tears. He shouldn't spend his last days worrying about what will happen to it. And soon, this company will be all I have left of him. Assuming I actually manage to hold on to the damn thing.

Personal sentiment aside, T&C also employs over six thousand people. Six thousand lives that will be turned upside-down if our rivals take over.

Fuck. I can't believe I'm even considering this ridiculous contract.

But my career is everything to me. It always has been. While other girls enjoyed normal social lives, I studied for hours every night. While they picked out homecoming dresses and sneaked booze from their parents' liquor cabinets, I did internships. While they rushed sororities, I co-chaired my university's Women Entrepreneurs Club. I aced every single one of my undergrad and MBA classes. No partying and barely any dating. I never coasted on Dad's reputation; ever since I was old enough to understand what a huge responsibility waited in my future, I wanted to be ready for it.

Well, I'm ready now. I've worked hard all my life, and I've earned the right to prove myself as head of Tate & Cane. I'm confident that I can fill Dad's shoes.

I can't let Dad down. I can't let my younger self down. This company is mine; the thought of losing it to a rival is even worse than the thought of Noah making suggestive comments at me for the rest of my life.

This company can't slip through my fingers, so I won't let it—even if that means I have to partner with Noah. Not just partner, but dear God, *marry* the son of a bitch. Our fathers must have gone temporarily insane when they wrote their wills. Then again, they always did have weird, old-fashioned ideas about dating and courtship.

But no situation is impossible. If I can just calm down and think clearly, an optimal solution will emerge. Any seemingly impossible goal can be managed by breaking it down into bite-sized component tasks.

I breathe deeply to calm myself and try to let my training take over.

Camryn has made two important points. First, both

Noah and I want to save Tate & Cane Enterprises. This company is our birthright, our fathers' legacy—and its employees are our responsibility. And second, this marriage is just another form of legal partnership. Which means it's a contract open to negotiation.

Yes, it royally sucks that I'm not marrying for love. My closet romantic side cringes at the thought. But I try to set aside as much emotional baggage as I can. Not every marriage has to be like a Hollywood romance, after all. Noah and I don't need to be in love with each other to successfully co-pilot a company.

The $100 billion question here is: How well would we work together?

Can we even get along? Will our partnership be stable and productive? Or will it implode . . . taking Tate & Cane down with us?

This decision doesn't rest entirely on my shoulders. Our fathers have always said that we're stronger together—that's why they paired us off in the first place. So Noah ought to do some heavy lifting too. In fact, I could argue that it's his job to convince me, since he's already on board.

So, let him make his sales pitch. Let him prove himself to me. Let him demonstrate how and why this relationship could actually succeed. I'll do my part too—I'll try to maintain good faith and stay receptive to the idea of us becoming friends. But I'm not the type to commit to something unless I know I can follow through. If I'm going to marry Noah, then by God, I want to *win* at it.

The end of my inner debate must show on my face, because Camryn reaches across the table to squeeze my hand.

"I'm going to order us dessert."

"I love you," I say on a sigh. Even with my newfound determination, I'll need some serious chocolate to get through this.

"For what it's worth, I think you're really brave."

I force a smile. "Thanks."

Grumbling to myself, I fish my phone out of my purse and call Dad to schedule another meeting with Noah and Prescott. I have to give them my answer as soon as possible.

• • •

Late that afternoon, almost the close of the business day, I open the same conference room door I walked through yesterday. Nobody turns in response; the three men seated at the table have already looked up at the sound of my footsteps in the hall.

Noah's crooked smile is just a little bit too smug. *What was that you said earlier? Something about not marrying me?* it seems to gloat. *How's that humble pie taste?*

A muscle tenses in my jaw. He didn't even have to say a word and I'm already irritated all over again. Goddamn it, he's so annoyingly attractive—with his charcoal-gray suit, crisp white shirt, and merlot-colored tie, all expertly tailored to fit his six-foot-two frame— and the fact that he can get under my skin so easily just annoys me even more.

His entire demeanor screams confidence. From his deep, inquisitive eyes that see too much, to his strong hands with neatly trimmed nails, to the thick column of his throat that bobs when he smirks at me. He's the thing my teenage fantasies were made of. Woodsy male scent. Muscular, yet trim frame. A quick wit that always finds a way to pull me into a debate.

Ignoring the pounding of my heart, I force my eyes away from Noah and address the room. "Thank you all for reconvening on such short notice. I have a proposal to make."

"I thought that was my job," Noah interjects.

Pointedly ignoring his joke, I explain. "I'll sign the inheritance contract at the end of the month . . ."

Everyone blinks at me. Dad and Prescott look pleasantly surprised. Noah's annoying smile is gone, replaced with a slightly furrowed brow.

"But only," I continue, "if Noah can show me that a relationship between us could work. After all, Tate & Cane's fate hinges on our ability to cooperate as both business partners and spouses."

"A trial period?" Dad asks.

"You could describe it like that. I also think that getting to know each other better will help the company's public image. We need to make our relationship believable; it'll look strange if nobody ever sees us together before we marry."

It's also a chance to dip my toes in before diving straight into the deep end. An attempt to inject a little normality into a deeply abnormal situation.

But I don't say that part out loud. I don't want to admit right now that marriage still scares me a little. Not with Noah blinking curiously at me, and Prescott looking frustrated at the prospect of even further delays.

Noah finally speaks up. "So, essentially, you're asking me to date you."

I nod at him. "Yep, that's the idea. At least take me out for a drink before I consider taking your name." I look straight at him, waiting to see his reaction before I hit him with my next clause. "Oh, and another thing. Refrain from having sex . . . with anyone."

Chapter Three

Noah

She wants me to woo her?

Of all the scenarios I imagined—from the most likely, where Olivia rips up the contract, to the even crazier, where she actually signs it—this wasn't one of them.

She's laid down her own stipulations, ensuring that I'll have to work to win her over. Though I probably should have expected a curveball. This is Olivia Cane, after all.

"If there are no further questions, I should get back to work," Olivia says. When nobody responds, she turns and struts out of the conference room, her round ass swaying as her heels click across the floor. The door swings shut.

"That was interesting," I say under my breath.

Fred stops beside me as I stand, trying to process

what just happened. "It sounds like the ball's in your court, son. But don't worry. I know you can pull this off."

"Thanks." I nod, then take off toward her office. She doesn't get to drop a bomb like that and then saunter away.

She's inside, perched in her cream-colored leather chair, stilettos kicked off under her desk. Her toenails are painted light blue, and she's tapping her foot in time to whatever tune she's humming. Something on her computer screen has her complete attention.

Startled at the sound of the door opening, she looks up, her wide crystal-blue eyes finding mine. "Did you need something? I have work to do."

She mentioned us going for a drink. Which is perfect, considering I need to prove how compatible we can be. But first, I need her to see something. This isn't just some game; I need her to understand exactly what's at stake if we don't succeed.

"Come with me. There's something I need to show you."

I tug her up from her desk chair, allowing her a moment to slip her delicate feet back into her heels, then tow her from the office before she can argue.

"Where are you taking me?"

I grunt and mumble, "You'll see."

"Don't be such a caveman; use your words."

"We're going to the mail room."

She scoffs. "What on earth for?"

I don't answer, just punch the button for the elevator. We cruise down to the basement floor of the building with an eerie silence hanging around us. When the doors open to the basement, I take a deep breath.

"Ahh . . . you smell that?" I grin at her.

Her mouth turns down into a frown. "Mildew?" Her gaze darts around the large open space stacked with boxes. "The health department would have a field day down here."

This is my favorite place in the whole building, so I don't take too kindly to Olivia turning up her nose at it.

"Don't be such a grouch. Come on."

I lace my fingers with hers once again and tug her farther down the fluorescent-lit hallway. When we reach the mail room, I wonder for a moment if Rosita is on her break.

"Now, what is it that you wanted to show me?" Olivia raises her eyebrows and places one hand on her hip, obviously not impressed.

Wide shelves line all four walls. They're numbered with the corresponding floors of the building and hold various envelopes and packages. It's not a high-tech operation, but it gets the job done.

"Not what, but who." I tip my chin toward the Latina cheerfully humming a tune to herself. Rosita's back is to us as she sorts mail at the far end of the room.

"Rosita," I call out.

She swivels around, clearly not expecting anyone, and her shoulder-length hair swings. A look of surprise is painted across her pleasant features, especially her large dark brown eyes, and a hint of pink comes to her round cheeks.

Rosita immigrated here from Mexico when she was just eighteen, taught herself English, and worked hard to support her growing family. Now, she's a force to be reckoned with.

A company of this size usually employs a mailroom staff of three to four people. But Rosita said they'd just get in her way, so she runs the whole operation herself. She took ownership of both the position and the space, and made it hers—even hung cheery posters on the wall. One of a monkey dancing. Another of bright orange poppies.

"*Mi amor!*" she cries, already heading toward us. "*Abrazo.*" She opens her arms to me, expecting our customary hug.

"*Gracias, Mamacita,*" I reply, giving her a light squeeze.

It's the same way she's been greeting me for the past six years. I know about a whopping four words of Spanish, but I always use them with her. I want her to feel at home, I guess.

Coincidentally, Rosita and I started work here on the same day. We even attended orientation together. I was a fresh college grad, still wet behind the ears, and Rosita, fifteen years my elder, was skeptical about the owner's son. Unlike Olivia, I haven't worked here since I could walk. I had other jobs during college and made a point of interning at another firm so I could see how the competition worked.

When I met her, I thought Rosita might assume I was some rich, privileged punk who didn't have to earn his paycheck. It made me all the more determined to prove her wrong. And Dad always was big on learning the ropes from the ground up, anyway. So for my first two weeks at Tate & Cane, I began working right alongside Rosita in the mail room.

It was during that time we cemented our relationship. We delivered packages and memos side by side, and shared jokes and stories. But when I really fell in love was when she shared her empanadas with me at lunch.

Rosita's eyes widen slightly as they swing from mine to Olivia's. "Miss Cane," she says, her voice soft and quizzical. It's not every day the CEO's daughter wanders down to the mail room.

"Please, call me Olivia," she says, correcting Rosita with a smile meant to ease. "It's nice to meet you."

Everyone at the company knows Olivia, even if they haven't met.

"Did you ... need something?" Rosita looks between me and Olivia again.

I shake my head. "Nope. Just came to say hello."

Rosita's posture relaxes and she smiles. "Did you get my invite for Maria's birthday party?"

"Of course. Two weeks from Saturday, right? It's already on my calendar."

"Have you had lunch yet?" She smiles and reaches out to smooth one hand over my silk tie. "I worry, you know."

I smile. "I've eaten. Thank you."

Sometimes when I'm busy, I've been known to skip lunch—that is, until Rosita forces herself into my office with a sandwich from the deli down the street. It's like she can sense when I've missed a meal. She often blurs the line between coworker, friend, and mother.

I've brought Olivia down here today because I want her to see there's more to this company than what the numbers say. Some things can't be learned from a spreadsheet. The perspective Olivia has perched in her corner office chair all day is quite different from the perspective one gets on the ground floor of this operation.

Standing here, looking into Rosita's rich mahogany eyes and feeling the warmth and care that pours from her very soul, it's impossible for us not to be aware of the importance of our responsibility. We can't fail at this. If we fail, we take all these people down with us.

And I, for one, won't let that happen.

After pleasantries are exchanged, Olivia and I head back toward the elevator.

"She's important to you, isn't she?" Olivia asks.

"Very."

She nods, looking contemplative.

I check my watch as we step inside the elevator and let out a sigh. Olivia looks as overwhelmed as I feel. We've been under a mountain of stress lately, and I have a feeling it's only going to get more intense.

"Today was unexpected," I say. "Just like that, after weeks of negotiation, you're actually going to consider this, huh?"

"I will do this on my terms, *if* and *when* I'm ready, Noah. Consider the next few weeks a trial period."

"That will be easy, sweetheart."

"Oh, it won't be easy," she says, correcting me. "And don't call me sweetheart."

"Are you sure about that, Mrs. Tate?"

"I told you not to call me that, either."

"I know. You told me to take you out for a drink before you'll consider taking my name." I smirk at her. "Which I think is an excellent fucking idea. Brilliant, in fact."

I coax my first smile from her and feel like thumping my chest. Although I have a desk full of work to get back to, the idea of sitting across from Olivia and hearing her tell me about this supposed trial period sounds like a lot more fun. Time to push a little harder.

"It's five o'clock somewhere, you know."

"We've had a lot going on. I think we could use a cocktail," she says, amazing me that she actually agreed.

"I'll meet you in the lobby in fifteen?" I know she'll never agree to leave without wrapping up the last of her e-mails.

"Sure."

Then I watch her ass as she saunters away toward her office.

• • •

Once we're seated at the elegant Stanton Room, a swanky bar across the street from our office building, Olivia and I place our order with the waitress—a vodka martini, extra dirty for her, and a Scotch on the rocks for me.

"Extra dirty, huh?" I wink at her.

"Surprised?" There's a hint of a smile on her lips.

"That the straitlaced Olivia Cane likes it extra dirty? Why, yes, I am."

"Don't overthink it, Noah. I'd hate to see you burst a brain cell."

I scowl at her. If there's one thing Olivia and I do well, it's banter. And though she'd like to believe otherwise, sexual tension runs rampant just below the surface.

I lean in toward her, my elbows on the table. "So, how will all this work, exactly? Me and you? I just like to be clear on expectations so I can exceed them."

Her gaze is cool. Not icy, at least, but still a long way from where I want her. "Well, I haven't put a lot of thought into it yet, but you'll have to win me over. Show me that this crazy thing could actually work."

If there's one thing I know about Olivia, it's that she refuses to fail. Something tells me that with everything that's on the line, Olivia needs to know I won't fuck up and embarrass her as a husband. We have to work together, live together, and actually pull off this whole coupledom in a big way.

"So you said you want to date? I don't date, Snowflake."

"Winning over doesn't necessarily mean dating."

She takes a sip from her martini glass and sets it down with an inquisitive look on her delicate features. She may look like your average, sweet girl next door, but at her core, Olivia is a ballbuster. A total triple threat. Sexy, intelligent, and talented. Which is perfect, seeing as those are the qualities I always dreamed my future wife would possess. Well, those, along with a tight—

Olivia clears her throat, interrupting my train of thought. *Fuck.*

"Winning over means that we can be in the same room together without ripping each other's throats out."

I nod. "Okay, we'll be civilized about it."

"Fine," she says. "And we should figure out what the hell we have in common."

I think we already know what we have in common—and to my understanding, it's a long list. But I'll go by whatever definition she wants. I'll win no matter what it is.

"Seeing as we have to put on a show, I agree. I should know a bit about my future fiancée," I say. "For instance, your favorite sexual position . . ."

She coughs and sputters, choking on the olive in her drink. For a minute there, I think I'm going to have to perform the Heimlich maneuver, until she swallows the damn thing and glares at me.

"What does that have to do with anything?" she croaks out, her voice still hoarse.

I chuckle. "Settle down. I just want to know how to please my future wife, is all."

"You can please me by buckling down and getting to work at the office instead of taking those three-martini lunches you favor."

"Darling?" I blink at her. Since I've been told by more than one ex-girlfriend that my eyelashes are enviable, I'm hoping it has the exaggerated effect I'm going for. "We were supposed to be discussing what we have in common."

"Right. Well . . ." She begins listing items on her fingers. "Summering in the Hamptons. Working at Tate & Cane, obviously. Our families are friends."

"We both lost our mothers," I point out.

Her gaze drops to the table in front of her, but I don't feel bad. It's just a fact of life, one we've discussed before, and I'd rather skip the superficial bullshit and get down to a real level.

"Yes. What else?" She drums her fingers on the table.

"I, for one, like anal. You?"

Damn it. Again with the choking. I stand and pat my future fiancée's back until her airway clears.

"Another drink?" I ask, noticing that hers is now empty.

She looks flustered that she downed it so quickly, but signals to the waitress for another round.

"I know what I'm getting myself into, Noah. Besides, my focus is going to be on saving this company, not pretending to be the happy little wife to my fake husband."

"Correction." I lean closer. "Soon to be *real* husband. I'll win you over, Snowflake. This *will* happen."

Chapter Four

Olivia

Win me over, Noah says. *Real husband.*

There's nothing real about this. He can call this trial period "dating" if he wants, but all I'm after is reassurance that we'll mesh as co-CEOs. No need to confuse the issue with love or sex, no matter how dangerously attractive he is. I just have questions that need answers.

For instance, what made him take me to the mail room today? He practically dragged me downstairs. Whatever his reason, he thinks it's important. Was he trying to give me a reality check, remind me that I'm not the only one with problems around here, so I should suck it up? Or was he just trying to show me his warm fuzzy side?

If the latter was his goal, it kind of worked. I have to admit that Rosita and Noah act adorable together. Almost like mother and son. The most stone-faced person on Earth would smile at their affection. And it's not like I ever thought Noah lacked integrity or kindness, just the finer points of self-discipline. I have plenty of evidence to believe that getting closer to him won't be so bad.

But while I can hazard guesses all day, I want to hear Noah's explanation in his own words. And we're overdue for a topic change anyway.

"Why did you introduce me to Rosita?" I ask.

"To show you what's at stake."

Despite fully anticipating it, his holier-than-thou tone still makes my lip curl. "As if I had no clue about the gravity of our situation. That's the whole point of doing this trial period—to see how well we can play ball together before committing to a team-up. I'm doing my best to become friends with you, so . . ."

He tilts his head with a half smile. "Just friends? I've got my sights set a little higher."

Gee, I never would have guessed, what with his constant attempts to steer the conversation toward sex.

I quirk one eyebrow in skepticism. "Friendship is all we need to pull this thing off. And we're pretty much starting from square one … I would call us acquaintances, at best. Don't you think you're being a little overambitious?"

"Nope," he replies, cocky smile still firmly in place.

I roll my eyes. "Wow. Your arrogance truly has no limits."

"If I can put my money where my mouth is …" His lustful smirk makes it clear exactly where he'd like to put his mouth. "Then it's not arrogance. Just confidence."

"What makes you think I would want more with you, anyway? You aren't exactly my type."

I expect him to just give me a knowing look, or maybe toss back some mild innuendo. What I absolutely did not expect was, "Because I have a nine-inch cock."

I almost choke on my martini for a third time. I splutter, "Is that number supposed to impress me?" Does he seriously expect me to believe that kind of porn-star bullshit?

"It's the truth," he purrs, leaning slightly closer. "And I know how to use it. Along with my tongue, my hands . . . just ask any woman I've been with."

"Spare me the play-by-play. You've fucked half of New York City. I'm willing to believe that you learned *something* in the process."

"First, I haven't fucked half of New York. Believe it or not, I'm pretty discerning. Second, instead of hearsay, why not just see for yourself?"

I give him a skeptical look. "You want to show me your dick?"

"If it'll help convince you." He drains the last drops of his Scotch and stands up. "Come on, let's go."

I stare after him as he walks away.

Is he serious? He's just going to whip it out? I look around to see if anyone is watching me, then I get up and follow him to the bar's back hallway, near the restrooms, unable to comprehend why the hell I'm humoring him. *This is ridiculous.*

Once we're safely in a private corner, Noah undoes

his belt, opens his fly . . . and pulls out a fucking fire hose.

Holy mother of God. My hands fly to my mouth. I want to gasp in shock, but there's no way I'm giving him the upper hand.

He was right. His cock is nothing short of massive, and it's not even fully erect right now. Nine inches may actually be a conservative estimate of what it might look like hard. He must destroy men's egos every time he walks into a locker room. And I don't even want to think about what he destroys with women . . .

"Meh. I've seen bigger," I force out, fighting to maintain my composure.

Noah chuckles. "I don't think so, sweetheart."

"Well, th-that *monster* is not coming anywhere near my uterus. No, thank you. I prefer to keep my organs intact."

Noah's grin widens. "I doubt that, but just to be on the safe side, I'll ease it in nice and slow. Piece of cake. Plus, you've got good health insurance, right?"

"That is not funny, Noah. Now, put that thing away or I'll remove it."

I try to sound stern, but my shaking voice and bright red cheeks surely give me away. Why the hell can't I stop staring?

He chuckles—yeah, the jerk can definitely see right through me—but he obliges, tucking the beast back into its lair.

I try to compose myself as we head back to the bar. Once seated, as coolly as I can, I say, "This doesn't change my opinion, you know."

"Really? Not at all?" He raises his eyebrows.

Of course, seeing his dick made an impression. How could it not? But I'll be damned if I stroke his . . . ego any more than I already have.

"Look, this whole dating thing is just to prove that we can live and work together. You don't need to go for extra credit."

"But what if I want to?"

"Noah . . ."

"Would you at least be willing to try it? We could start super slow. Set strict limits. Like, say . . ." He waves his hand vaguely. "Nothing past first base."

"A trial run within a trial run," I say slowly, tasting the idea. I'm a little skeptical, but I guess it wouldn't hurt to fool around a little. I can always call *game over* if I'm feeling underwhelmed.

"Exactly. Just testing the waters. We can pretend we're back in high school or something."

I take a long sip of my drink, considering. Then I reply, "I'll think about it."

Chapter Five

Noah

Game on.

Chapter Six

Olivia

Oh, joy. The renowned marketing firm of Wesson, Burke and Barsol has sent a vulture. And for some godforsaken reason, our board of directors agreed to let him blow hot air through his yellowing teeth for an hour and call it a "negotiations meeting."

Tate & Cane has been rivals with WBB from day one. So, naturally, its CEO started salivating as soon as he smelled blood. Officially, the vulture is an "acquisitions representative," but the formality of that title is just a smoke screen. He's here to try to pick the carcass before it's even stopped moving.

Holding back an aggravated sigh, I shift in my seat at the conference table. I don't have time for this bullshit; I have an entire company to rehabilitate. "Meeting with potential buyers" is about as far down my to-do list as it gets. Especially since I have no idea what this jerk is even doing here, other than wasting everyone's time and sending my blood pressure through the roof. It'll be ninety days—no, eighty-six now—until the board even decides whether they want to sell Tate & Cane, let alone who they'll sell it to.

Maybe all this stress is just making me hysterical, but I can't keep my mouth from twitching at the sight of the rep's hair. He has, without a doubt, one of the greasiest, scraggliest, saddest comb-overs I've ever seen. And I've been part of the elite corporate world since I was old enough to hold Dad's hand at company dinners. Trust me, I know my bad comb-overs.

How appropriate . . . a bald vulture. Maybe I should check his hands for talons. I take a sip of coffee just to hide my smirk.

Dad clears his throat to interrupt the rep's rambling. "Excuse me, Mr. Valmont, but I'd just like to clarify a few points."

The rep blinks a few times, as if he's forgotten that there were other people in the room. "Yes, Mr. Chairman?"

"Your purchase offer seems very low. Our company's total value has been estimated at over twice this figure. And your planned policy changes are quite extensive." Dad peers over his glasses at his copy of WBB's proposal. "Not to mention the universal layoffs—surely you don't have to fire *all* of our current employees?"

"Freshly acquired companies always undergo some restructuring." The rep adjusts his tie. "It's standard industry practice, as I'm sure you already know. Buyers have to make sure that their new asset fits into their, ah . . . their corporate culture."

"Of course," Dad says. "Just making sure the board understands."

Oh yeah, the board understands, all right. Nobody sitting at the conference table has even the trace of a smile.

I steal a glance at Noah, who's sitting just to my left. He looks absolutely miserable—brow furrowed, lips pressed tight, shoulders tensed around his ears. His body language is shocking, especially for a man who's normally as cool as a cucumber.

A pang of sympathy tightens my chest. I feel the unexpected urge to reach out and take Noah's hand. It's gone as quickly as it comes, but the underlying ache remains. God knows I'm not his biggest fan, but with potential buyers in the room, my choice is a no-brainer. Of course I'll stand firm with Noah. After all, the enemy of my enemy is my friend.

Except Noah isn't just the enemy of my enemy. We really are on the exact same side here. We're both doing this for the same reasons—for our fathers, our futures, for all the people who depend on T&C's jobs to feed their families. And we stand to lose the same high stakes. I know Noah won't give up without a fight.

The ache in my chest deepens, softens into something that feels almost like loyalty. Solidarity.

Noah's eyes flick over to mine; he must have sensed my gaze on him. As subtly as I can, I incline my head and give him a small, tight-lipped smile. I don't want the vulture or even Dad to see what I'm doing. This message is meant only for the two of us.

Don't worry. We're going to outsmart these fuckers. I swear on our mothers' graves, we'll win.

The vulture gets up from his chair with a creak.

Noah looks back at him, breaking our brief connection.

"My employers urge you to consider committing to this sale as soon as possible," Valmont says. "Our offer is quite generous, and it won't be on the table indefinitely."

"We'll be sure to keep WBB in mind if we ever decide to sell," Dad replies smoothly, ignoring the man's limp-dicked attempt at a threat. "Thank you for coming to visit us today."

I give a tiny mental cheer. *Hell yeah! Dad said if, not when.* Small victories.

The rep doesn't look impressed by Dad's carefully neutral non-smile. Probably because he knows that "we'll keep you in mind" is just a polite translation of "go piss up a rope." But what did WBB expect, trying to sneak in ahead of the competition like this?

The meeting is adjourned. Dad excuses himself—probably to wash up after shaking the rep's slimy hand. As I head back toward my office, Noah catches up with me in the hall.

"You doing okay?" he asks.

Noah's asking *me* that? He was the one who looked on the verge of strangling that prick back there.

"Yeah, I'm fine." I sigh. "Just pissed off."

"I thought you were always pissed off," he teases.

"Only when I'm around you," I fire back automatically, but without any real feeling. I'm still too distracted and stressed out.

Noah just chuckles, as if we're playing tennis instead of trading insults. I have to admit, his laugh is a nice sound—and I like seeing him this way a lot better than what I saw at the meeting. Even if he can be an annoying little shit when he's cheerful.

We walk together for a minute, with only the soft pad of our footsteps and the low murmur of office chatter in the background.

"What about you?" I finally ask. "Are you okay?"

"I feel a lot better now that I'm talking to you."

More flirting. Why does he have to keep messing with me like that? And why does my stomach always have to give a little flip in response? I hate how easily he can make me react.

"But back there, not so much," Noah continues. "I thought I was going to punch that asshole in his smug face. This company isn't just numbers on a spreadsheet. These are people's lives they're planning to fuck up."

"Right . . . like Rosita. You care so much about her." From yesterday, I already knew that they were close, but seeing Noah get so upset really drives home how important she is to him.

His sigh is deep and troubled. "How could I not? She's one of the sweetest people to ever walk the Earth. And she has a family to worry about."

Suddenly he stops and faces me, the corners of his mouth picking up again, but his eyes telling me he's still troubled about the meeting and what we learned. "Well, this is me. I guess it's time to get back to work."

I look around and see he's right—we're standing outside his office door.

Here already? When did we walk all this way? Time must have flown by.

I feel an odd twinge of disappointment, unwilling to end this conversation yet. I don't know what else to say; I just feel like talking to Noah a little longer.

Or maybe I just don't want to be alone right now. I want to hang on to that moment we shared at the meeting. The reassuring, invigorating sense that we're fighting by each other's sides. Allies in the trenches. *Misery loves company, I guess . . .*

But my to-do list is too long for me to pay attention to such a tiny, nebulous feeling. So I shake off my reluctance and nod good-bye at Noah.

"I'll see you later."

"Not too much later, I hope." With a wink, Noah disappears into his office.

Gah . . . tummy flip, right on cue. Screw him—no, wait, don't screw him. I mean, forget him. And his monster penis. I have a million things to do and I've already wasted half the day.

I turn on my heel and head for my office. Maybe my feelings will settle down once I start working. I'll bury myself in tough financial problems, get a good flow going, and let all distractions slip away.

But the idea of solitude, normally blissful, still rubs me the wrong way for some reason. And as my mind wanders, so do my feet. I find myself in front of Dad's door instead of my own.

I let myself inside his office, savoring the church-like silence, the calming scents of wood polish and coffee and paper. For as long as I can remember, I've always felt at home in this office. I was practically raised here, after all. I've read every volume of every book and business journal on its shelves. I know every inch of this room, and its familiarity soothes my jangled nerves.

The door opens again with a soft click, and Dad says, "I knew I'd find you here."

I can hear the smile in his voice without even turning around. Which is good, because I'm suddenly too tired to do anything more than breathe.

"Something you want to talk about?"

Bypassing his mahogany desk and the imposing throne behind it, Dad sits on the squat leather armchair by the coffee table. I take the armchair on its other side.

It makes the same awkward farting noise it's made for the past eighteen years.

"No. I mean . . ." I sigh. "Maybe."

I don't even know what I need right now. My thoughts are still flying in all directions: The vulture, somehow dismissive and hungry at the same time. The tense misery in Noah's pose. Dad's careworn face, its wrinkles deepening by the day. The board's insane deadline. All the work that lies ahead of me—of us. The mere word "us," the idea that soon, I'll become a *we* instead of a *me*.

But maybe that isn't such a terrible fate. Partnership has its good points as well as bad. I've seen that synergy firsthand, in the way that Dad and Bill Tate led this company together.

And I remember the glance I shared with Noah back in the conference room. That split second of mutual understanding, where I saw straight through Noah's eyes. I could tell exactly how he felt—alone, overwhelmed—and suddenly I didn't feel so alone and overwhelmed myself. Putting on a brave face for him bolstered my own courage. Even now, I feel stronger and calmer for having smiled at him.

It's actually kind of amazing just how powerful one glance can be. How much it can communicate. How it can pull me out of despair, even slow down my heartbeat ... or speed it up. Like what happened between us in the hall a few minutes ago. Or the meeting where he kissed my hand.

For God's sake, is my libido ever going to shut up? Now is really not the fucking time. *Ugh, wait. Poor choice of words.*

"You still there, sweetie?" Dad asks.

I blink back to reality. *Shit, I got lost in thought again.* My thoughts are pretty easy to get lost in these days.

"Sorry. I just ... I don't really know where to start." That's definitely no lie.

"I'll pour us some coffee." He leans forward with a grunt.

"No, Dad, don't get up. I can do it." I stand up and walk to the sideboard to turn on the single-cup machine.

He lets out a small sigh through his nose. "I know

I'm no spring chicken anymore, but—"

"It's okay. I don't mind."

Dad is proud and I don't want to make him feel helpless, but I know damn well how much pain and fatigue he's dealing with. And to be honest, I'm desperate to get off my ass and *do* something. Anything at all. I just need action.

So I busy myself with the coffee. Hazelnut for me, Colombian dark roast for Dad. Sweetener but no cream for me, cream but no sweetener for Dad. The ritual itself is almost as soothing as the rich scents that steam from our mugs.

I hoped that talking would come easier like this, with my hands occupied and my back turned so I don't have to worry what crosses my face—or what might cross Dad's. But the words that leap from my mouth take us both by surprise.

"Why did Bill Tate do this to us?"

Dad sighs again. This one is loud, heavy, rising from deep within his chest.

My mouth snaps open to apologize. But then I close it again. Because you know what? Even if I never intended to demand answers—fuck it, I really do want some. In fact, I have a right to them. I'm the one who was forced to choose between the frying pan and the fire, after all.

"I'm sorry, sweetie," Dad says. "We never imagined it would turn out this way. We wrote those clauses together, into both our wills, because we wanted to keep T&C in the family, and we knew you kids were meant to be together."

I nod a little impatiently as I hand him his coffee mug and sit down with mine. I already know most of this part of the story. A joint venture, in more than one sense of the word.

He takes a sip. "Still, we tried to make sure that you had other options. If you and Noah didn't want to marry by the time we retired—a day we thought was far in the future—then control would default to the board. And even so, you wouldn't lose the company. You would have been granted board seats and paid highly from T&C's profits. So we didn't make this decision lightly. But we never anticipated . . ."

"That there would be no profits," I say softly. And maybe no company at all.

"Right. Because everything just happened all at once, with the worst possible timing. Bill's early death. My cancer . . . and how fast it advanced. T&C lagging behind its competition, falling into the red. The board's crisis of faith." Another deep sigh. "We always thought you kids would have so many more years to come around to the idea."

I know how hard Dad has tried to save this company on his own. He's worked until his body physically won't let him anymore. By the time he admitted defeat, the problem had reached do-or-die proportions. I'm not angry with him for that, because I know I wouldn't have done any different. We're cut from the same proud, stubborn cloth.

Dad puts down his barely touched coffee with a soft *clunk*. "I'm not going to be around forever, sweetie."

I look up, startled at the topic change. He suddenly

looks so haggard, it breaks my heart.

"I . . . I know that, Dad, but—"

"You marrying Noah isn't just for the company's sake. Who cares about a company if my little girl is unhappy? I trust Noah to take care of you."

"I don't need taking care of," I say automatically.

"Everyone needs someone around. I'm not talking about money or power . . . I'm talking about love. A listening ear, a shoulder to cry on. A partner who shares life's burdens. If I know you have that, sweetie, then I can rest a lot easier."

I swallow a lump in my throat, washing it down with hot coffee. I don't want to think about Dad resting.

"Despite everything, I still believe that you and Noah belong together," Dad continues. "You were made for each other. And you'll need each other's strength for what lies ahead. Bill Tate's will has just given things a little push in the right direction."

I look down into my mug, the dark liquid glinting under the fluorescent lights. "This still just feels so . . .

unreal. I have no idea what to expect. What's it like to be married?"

I'm not even sure what kind of answer I want to hear. What cute anecdote or pearl of wisdom could possibly reassure me. *Everything will be okay. Marriage won't swallow up your whole life. You can still be yourself—a businesswoman first and a wife second.*

"Well, in my experience, it was wonderful." Dad smiles fondly. "Your mom was the greatest thing that ever happened to me. My rock, my sunshine, my best friend. We weren't two halves of a whole, we were each our own person, and that's what made us so amazing when we joined together." He shakes his head. "I'm no poet, so all I can say is . . . it was magic."

Magic, huh? I'll have to take his word for it. My only long-term boyfriend turned out to be a manipulative narcissist, and I've never gotten close enough to any other man for the kind of deep bond that my father is trying to describe.

Dad leans forward in the chair, elbows on his knees and fingers steepled. "I know the circumstances are far from ideal, sweetie. But try to at least give Noah a shot.

I'd never put you in a situation I didn't think you could handle. You're my baby girl . . . I just want to see you with a good man. And that man is Noah."

I don't quite share Dad's glowing opinion of Noah. Not yet—although hopefully that will change by the end of this month. But I remember how fiercely he cares about Rosita and her family's welfare. There's no mistaking the strength of his conviction.

If nothing else, I know I can count on Noah to step up to the plate and fight for T&C. I can trust him to work just as hard as I will. Which is good, because we'll be spending the next three months in Overtime Hell together.

At least I'll have some eye candy to ogle during all those late nights at the office. But now that I know about that telephone pole between his legs, I don't know how I'll ever look at him the same way.

Heaven help me.

Chapter Seven

Noah

You know how men are supposed to be more direct and forceful, while women are gentler and more attuned to emotions? That's horseshit. As business partners, Olivia and I blur gender stereotypes. I'm the "face," the charismatic people-pleaser, while she's the get-shit-done powerhouse. Playing to our strengths lets us divide and conquer.

Of course, it doesn't hurt that men—especially stodgy, rich old farts—tend to listen better to other men. I can close deals over a round of golf, woo male and female clients alike, and generally sweet-talk my way through any situation. Which is exactly what I've spent this last week doing.

Today, though, I'm back in the office. And right now, I'm grinding my teeth at the sight of Harrison Ridgefield from the accounting department leering at Olivia's cleavage.

"Something I can help you with there, buddy?" I snap as I step into Olivia's office and stop right beside him.

His head jerks up and he smiles sheepishly, as if he knows he's been caught. "Oh. Hey, Noah. Didn't see you there," he says, his voice unsteady.

"That's because you were busy staring at my girlfriend's . . . *spreadsheets.*"

Olivia and I haven't announced our courtship yet, but rumor knows no bounds. The unofficial news has spread like fucking wildfire through our whole building.

Harrison swallows hard and takes a step back. "Congrats on all that, by the way."

My blank stare says *I'm on to you, prick.* I even puff out my chest a little for good measure. Harrison isn't a bad-looking guy. I hear the office gossip; I know he's the wet dream of at least a few of the ladies here. But I've got about two inches on his six-foot frame, and more muscle too.

"Well, it looks like you've got it covered here, Olivia." The douche bag treats her to a fond smile and steps away from her desk.

"Thanks, Harrison," Olivia says as she watches him leave.

"What are you doing?" I glare down at Olivia's monitor. There are pages and pages of data on her screen. I have no idea what it is—but I do know she looks stressed, and I want to fix it.

"Just trying to reconcile the invoices we sent clients last year with the actual dollars received." She taps a four-inch-thick stack of printouts on her desk. "Something feels off about it."

"Olivia . . ." I exhale slowly.

Her eyes jerk up to mine. "What?"

"You shouldn't be spending your time on menial shit like this. We have too much strategizing and brand-building to do to keep your head buried in busywork."

"Excuse me, Mr. Cranky-Pants, but 'burying my head' might end up saving us a fuck-ton of money." Her blue eyes burn brightly, and I know I'm in for a fight if I push too hard.

Well, too bad. I'll grab the tiger by the tail if that's what it takes to stop her.

"What I'm trying to say is that your talents are wasted on this. Your time is valuable. This is what I mean when I say you work too hard. Tasks like these need to be delegated. You don't have to do everything yourself."

"Harrison was helping me—"

I hold up one hand. "Harrison was enjoying the peep show. Nothing more." I make a point of letting my gaze drop slowly from hers down to the front of her blouse. The sight of the top of her firm, round breasts cradled in a delicate nude-colored bra makes my mouth water. I ignore the tingle at the base of my spine and the blood surging toward my groin, and take a deep breath.

Olivia's gaze jerks from mine down to her cleavage, and she hoists her shirt up higher. "Oh, for fuck's sake, he was not."

She is seriously delusional. Harrison has had a wicked crush on her for three years. And he's an underperforming ass, if you ask me.

"God, you're grumpy today. Why don't you go get one of those blow jobs you like from Jenni in HR?"

"Huh. I'm surprised you know about that." I enjoyed a handful of oral encounters from a nice admin assistant earlier this year, but all that is over.

"I know everything that goes on around here." She smirks.

Hell. "First of all, Jenni no longer works here."

"Oh, darn." She snaps her fingers in mock outrage.

"Secondly . . ." I lean my hip against her desk. "Even if she did, I'd have zero interest in seeing her lips around my cock right now."

"The infamous Noah Tate, not interested in chasing tail? Do I need to call you an ambulance?" she teases. "Or are you just having too much fun bugging me and keeping me away from work?"

My temper rising, I stand my ground. "Because I think of myself as a taken man now."

Her eyebrows dart up. "Are you serious? You're really not going to mess around?"

"Not with anyone who isn't you," I say smoothly.

"I—um . . . So, monogamy really is part of the deal?" she stammers. "I've had a standing Wednesday-night thing with a guy from the gym. Should I cancel that for the next little bit?"

My nostrils flare and I bite back my temper. "Hell yeah, it is, and yeah, you should. What goes for me, goes for you. You aren't to mess around with anyone who isn't me. I don't even want to think about another man touching what's *mine*." I lean down and growl the last part close to her ear.

She sucks in her breath, her pupils dilating, then composes herself. "As long as you know that this works both ways. If I find your totem pole next to anyone else, consider yourself castrated. Think Lorena Bobbitt, but without the whole finding-it part."

On the surface, her reaction isn't exactly promising. But I know that deep down, I've affected her. I've seen the way she looks at me when she doesn't think I'm watching.

"And for the record, I was kidding about the guy at

the gym, Noah."

Thank God, because I was already planning to go down to her gym after work and find the helpless fuck to punch him square in the kisser.

I step away from her desk and watch as Olivia's eyes narrow on my form. Tucking my hands into my pockets, I almost chuckle as her gaze follows the movement, her eyes drifting down to my crotch. But they dart up again and she lets out a frustrated huff.

"If you're so confident, how about we place a bet?" I ask.

"Name your terms."

She smirks at me, pretending to be unaffected. Too bad I know *exactly* the effect I can have on a woman when I turn on the charm.

I lean in closer. "I'll give you four days until you're begging for me to fill your hot little cunt," I murmur.

Her jaw drops, but she recovers quickly. "Not even in four years."

"I was going to say four hours, but I didn't want to

get cocky," I tease.

"Trust me. I can hold out for a *long* time." Olivia leans back in her desk chair, her pose casual and confident.

"Dry spell?"

She rolls her eyes. "Perpetually."

Fuck. That makes me want her so much more, knowing that she's all pent-up and unsatisfied.

"No battery-operated boyfriends."

Her gaze darkens. "Fine. No hand jobs either then."

My jaw tenses. Like that will happen. "There's always the trial run I proposed at happy hour."

She chews on her thumbnail. "I haven't had time to consider it yet, but I'll keep you posted when I decide."

A knock on the door grabs our attention. It's Fred.

"Hey, kids, time for the meeting."

Olivia checks her watch. "Be there right away,

Dad."

Knowing our conversation isn't even close to finished, I offer her a hand to assist her from her seat, bringing her eye level with me. "We'll finish this later, Snowflake."

She scoffs and struts down the hall in front of me, her gorgeous round ass swaying as she moves.

"Four days," I call to her as I catch up.

Chapter Eight

Olivia

Late the next afternoon, a knock on my office door startles me out of my work trance. "Come in," I say automatically.

The door cracks open and Dad pokes his head in. "Hey there, sweetie. Sorry if I'm interrupting anything, but could we talk for a minute in my office?"

I blink first at him, then at my computer screen before closing my laptop. "Sure, Dad. What do you need?"

"It's good news, I promise," is all he says.

I follow Dad to his office, where Noah is already sitting in one of the armchairs. He stands up when we walk in.

I glance between him and Dad suspiciously. *What fresh hell is this?*

Dad picks up a thin sheaf of papers from his desk.

"In all the recent hubbub, I forgot to tell you kids about my wedding gift." He hands over the document with a proud smile.

I scan the first page and my heart plummets. It's a signed lease for a furnished penthouse apartment in the heart of the city, its security deposit already paid, as well as first and last month's rent. And there's only one bedroom.

No way.

Realizing that I probably shouldn't just stand here in a stupor, I say, "Oh. Um . . . wow, Dad. This is so generous."

Dad chuckles and squeezes my shoulder. "Anything for my girl. I figured you two wouldn't have much time to go house-hunting right now, so I found you a place myself."

"Thank you very much, sir. I'm sure we'll love it," Noah interjects.

Jackass. He always knows exactly what to say, how to smooth over any situation. Whereas I'm struggling to remember how to breathe.

I force a tight-lipped smile at my dear, sweet future husband. "Yes. Noah, can we talk about this in your office? There's a lot of arrangements that need to be made."

• • •

As soon as we're alone with the door locked, I let my emotions burst free.

"What the hell are we going to do? He's already spent so much money, which T&C really can't afford, by the way, and he'll expect us to move in, and . . . what a clusterfuck!" I push my hands into my hair, not caring in the slightest that my perfectly coiffed bun just became a hot mess.

Noah holds up his hands. "Whoa, hey, calm down. Living together isn't really *that* big of a deal, is it?"

"Of course it's a big deal. I don't want to move in with anyone, especially not you."

He narrows his eyes. "What's that supposed to mean?"

"Oh, get over yourself. I'm sure you don't want to

live with me, either."

"As a matter of fact, I do."

I stare at him. "Why? Wouldn't that get in the way of your drinking and whoring?"

"I told you I wasn't going to do that anymore." Noah rakes his fingers through his hair irritably. "Okay, just listen to me for a second. Even if we ignore the fact that you're sex on legs and any sane man would give his left nut to spend a night with you—"

My laugh sounds ever so slightly hysterical. "You're seriously trying to flirt right now? Is that the only way you know how to communicate with women?"

"*Even if* we ignore that fact," he growls out, "we still have Tate & Cane's public image to consider. How bad will it look if we don't even live under the same roof?"

I rub my forehead, partly to ground myself and partly as an excuse to hide my expression. I can't cry in front of Noah. I don't cry, period.

Why am I even getting so upset? I already knew

we'd have to live together sooner or later. I've seen this coming since day one. That was one of the reasons I didn't want to sign the stupid contract in the first place. And I'm still feeling optimistic about Noah and our budding friendship. I'm not over the moon about having to share my private space with a roommate again, but I'll survive. Hell, it may even be fun. I have a lot of awesome memories from living with Camryn.

Really, Noah's right. It's not that big of a deal. But for some reason, it feels monumental. Like I'm about to lose yet another piece of myself.

I just hate surprises. Dad's wedding gift broadsided my composure and splattered all sorts of uncomfortable emotions everywhere. I need a moment to scrape myself back together.

"We don't really have a choice, Snowflake," Noah says. "Everyone—the media, our employees, our rivals, our stockholders—they all have to see us together. The starry-eyed young couple, poised to take over one of the nation's biggest companies. That's who we have to *be*."

I drop my gaze, chewing my lip hard. Finally, I admit, "Yeah, I know. You're right . . . our hands are tied. Sorry I flipped out for a minute there."

I half expect Noah to make some perverted joke about tied hands. But instead, he just touches me on the chin—the gentlest possible *hey, buck up.*

I meet his eyes as his fingers tilt my face to his. Can he tell how stupid and frustrated I feel? Why can't I hide anything from this man? Why can't I stop exposing my weak points?

Noah's sympathetic expression is both comforting and humiliating. I'm torn between the urge to relax, to let him support me, and the urge to jealously guard my dignity.

"No, I'm sorry too," Noah says in a much softer tone than before. "I know this situation really sucks for you, but we'll figure out ways to make it easier. Like our dads always said, we can accomplish anything if we're together."

I take a deep breath, then slowly let it out. Already my mind is starting to quiet. On the way back to my cool, collected self.

"You're right," I say. "We have to make this

courtship look real. So, living together will kill two birds with one stone—keep up appearances and let us get more familiar with each other."

Noah cocks his head with a salacious half smile. "Really? You've changed your mind about . . . ?"

"I haven't, so get your mind out of the gutter," I huff. Leave it to the immature horndog to purposely misunderstand me. "I meant that there's certain things we need to know about each other. Trivia, fun facts, stuff that could come up in conversation." We may have grown up together, but we haven't spent much time getting to know each other as adults.

"Like yesterday, when you just *assumed* I drink coffee." Noah raises his eyebrows in mock outrage.

"Right. If anyone had been watching, we would have looked like total strangers." Then I try to joke, "Although I still think that was a reasonable assumption on my part. I mean, who the hell drinks only tea? Tea is for relaxing; coffee is for waking up."

"Excuse me, Snowflake." Noah grins in the crooked way that I've come to learn means *game on.*

"You'd prefer me to be a twitchy addict like you? I've seen the sludge you drink. Pitch black . . . just like your heart."

"Actually, it's not," I reply coolly, smiling despite myself. "I take sweetener. Just because you can't see it doesn't mean it's not there."

"Fair point. We both have a few things to learn about each other." He thrusts his hands into his pockets and glances away for a second. "About the tea thing . . . my mom was English, and she really lived up to that particular stereotype. She loved 'a good cuppa.'" His voice lifts to imitate her lilting accent. "So I drink tea to . . . honor her memory, I guess you could say. It's my way of taking a moment every morning to think about her."

My jaw almost drops. His mom passed away when he was just ten. God, I remember that year like it was yesterday. It was such a sullen time. So dark and so quiet, like all the life had been sucked out of Noah and his dad in an instant.

I open my mouth to respond, but nothing comes out. I know his mom was British, but somehow it never dawned on me that he may have a special connection to her home country.

Noah shakes his head, looking a little embarrassed, and walks around me to perch on the edge of his desk. Leaving me to feel like a total bitch.

Biting my lip, I turn to face him again. "I'm so sorry. I didn't mean to make fun of you like that. I think your little tea-drinking memorial is . . . really sweet."

He shrugs. "Thanks, but don't worry about it. I wasn't offended. Especially since I know you've also lost your mom."

"Yeah, but I was practically an adult when she died. You were only ten. Just a little kid. You needed your mother." A sweet memory of him on her lap—when he was too big to fit, but not too big to want to be there—flashes through my brain.

"You could argue that being older just makes your pain fresher." Noah sighs. "Look, let's not get into some kind of weird Grief Olympics here, okay? Of course I miss Mum, but your experience wasn't better or worse than mine, just different. What matters is that we can understand each other."

He's always so smooth and confident about everything . . . even death. Before I can say anything more, Noah changes the subject.

"About the apartment—we should probably start spending nights there ASAP. I've got dinner plans with Sterling right now, but how about we meet back at the new place at . . ." He checks his watch. "How's eight?"

Considering all the preparations I need to make, I nod slowly. "Sure. That'll give me time to grab some food and pack." I turn to leave, but Noah interrupts me.

"Hey, Snowflake . . . can you do me one last favor?"

I stop, glancing back. "Yeah?"

"Could you smile again?"

For some reason, his directness flusters me so much that I blurt, "W-why should I?" Then I want the floor to swallow me up.

What the hell, Olivia? You sound like a bratty teenager.

"Because I don't want you to leave unhappy." Noah reaches out to brush my jaw with the back of his hand. The lightest, most fleeting touch, gone before I can say a word. "And because it looks good on you. I'd like to see that smile more often."

My face is on fire. I'm not sure how much of that heat is because I just embarrassed myself and how much is because of Noah's heated stare.

"I . . . I guess you'll get plenty of chances, now that we're living together." My attempt at a snappy retort comes out stuttering.

He inclines his head without breaking our gaze. "Great. I'm looking forward to it."

I swallow the boulder in my throat. *He's actually looking forward to it?*

"Hey, Noah?"

"Yes?" he says sweetly.

"Why do you call me Snowflake?"

He steps closer and runs one finger along my cheek, making my skin tingle in its wake. "Because you're just like a snowflake. Beautiful and unique, and with one touch you'll be wet."

Noah turns to leave, striding away with me staring after his broad shoulders and tight ass, with my mouth hanging open.

Dumbfounded, I shut the door behind me. Was that last comment meant to get a rise out of me? Or did he think I was really flirting?

Was I flirting? I thought I was just being bitter, but . . . maybe a tiny bit. I don't even know. And it doesn't help that my mind is still reeling from that bet we made yesterday.

• • •

I eat dinner alone at a little Italian bistro around the corner from the Tate & Cane building. I guess I was craving some comfort food. Spaghetti with meatballs and a glass of merlot do the trick nicely.

I take a cab home, and when I arrive, I e-mail my landlord to get the ball rolling on terminating my lease early. Then I start packing an overnight bag. I'll arrange for the rest of my clothes and other personal items to be delivered to our new place later. My furniture will just have to be sold.

One hour later, my little maroon suitcase is stuffed full. I have no excuse to linger further. But I do anyway—walking through slowly, looking at everything one last time.

This apartment has been the backdrop of my life for the past four years, ever since I got my undergrad degree and stopped rooming with Camryn. Everything within these walls is a product of my decisions and mine alone. I chose this place for its airy architecture, its honey-colored hardwood floors, even the blue-diamond tile pattern in the kitchen and bathroom. I bought every stick of furniture, striking my ideal balance between stylish and cozy. I decorated its walls with framed art prints that suited my tastes. I filled its fridge and cabinets with my favorite snacks. I cluttered the bathroom with my beauty products, not worrying about leaving space for anyone else's stuff. I organized everything according to the system that would best help me remember where I put it. Now . . . I can kiss all of that sovereignty good-bye.

Sure, I can bring a few more of my things to the penthouse, but so can Noah. He'll add his own unique flavor to our new home.

Our new home . . . I wonder how long it will take me to get used to that. And it's already fully furnished—which means no bringing my beloved squishy gray velvet sofa. Most importantly, there's only one bedroom. I won't have anywhere that's truly my domain anymore.

But Noah must feel the same way. He's also sacrificing the privacy and freedom of his bachelor pad. In fact, he has more to lose than me, since he actually had a sex life. And from what he said yesterday, it seems like he's serious about giving up his entire playboy lifestyle. Even though he's probably never been monogamous in his whole life.

Man, watching him try to keep it in his pants is going to be hilarious. And just what is his plan if I *do* take up with another man? Start a brawl like a couple of teenage punks?

I shake my head. That will never happen, anyway. Work is my whole life—I don't have time to invest in dating. And even though I'll never admit it to Noah, I don't have the stomach for one-night stands. I can't imagine myself enjoying physical intimacy without emotional intimacy. Unlike Noah, who seems to have zero problems whipping it out at the slightest provocation.

At least, he did until we started dating.

I seriously don't understand what's going through that man's head. All I wanted was for us to go from acquaintances to friends. Why does he have to push for overachievement? Why is he so determined to play the perfect boyfriend, even when nobody's around to witness his act? Why does he feel like he has to stay faithful to me?

Just to keep up appearances for the public? To gratify his male pride? Or because . . . he genuinely wants to woo me for real?

I realize I've been staring out the window for almost five full minutes. I haven't even been watching the dark, twinkling cityscape—moving lights for the cars, static ones for the offices working late or the families relaxing together. A glimpse into millions of people's lives, spread out in stars like a reflection of the night sky. I suddenly feel very small . . . and lonely.

It takes me a moment to recognize the feeling because I'm usually lonely in the abstract, daydreaming of a faceless fantasy lover. A hazy ache for human contact. Someone to brush his fingers through my hair and whisper sweet things in my ear. Someone to hold me and tell me everything will be okay. Someone to investigate when there's a noise in the night. Now, though, my loneliness is specific and sharp.

I want to see Noah.

He's the only person in the world who understands how I feel right now. Camryn can try to sympathize, and she's definitely done a lot to help me through this, but she's not down in the trenches with me. Noah is.

I'm not sure if I want to *talk* to him right now, but I at least want to see him. I want to know he's still there, by my side. I need to hear his optimism and see that smirk on his mouth to know that maybe, just maybe, I'll make it through this.

I pick up my suitcase, turn the lights off, and leave

my apartment for the last time.

• • •

Even at this time of night, Manhattan traffic isn't fun. As my cab crawls through the packed city streets, I suddenly get an idea.

"Is there a tea shop nearby?" I ask the cabbie.

He gives me a confused look in his rearview mirror. "What, like a café?"

"No, I mean a place where I can buy . . . equipment? Teapots and kettles and stuff."

He starts tapping his GPS screen. Fortunately, we're stopped at a red light, but I get the feeling that he wouldn't care if we weren't.

"About three blocks west," he says after a minute. "You got some shopping to do there?"

"Yes, please."

He promptly muscles into the right-turn lane, ignoring a few shouts and middle fingers from the other drivers, and speeds through. Somehow we arrive at the store without causing any vehicular manslaughter.

As I count out my fare, I say, "Can you wait for me? I shouldn't be more than twenty minutes."

He raises his bushy eyebrows. "That long? You sure? I'll have to drive around the block, and the meter's runnin' . . ."

"I can afford it." For now, anyway. Tate & Cane isn't totally underwater yet.

He shrugs. "Okay, lady, whatever you want."

I step out of the cab and he's gone before I reach the front door.

The tiny boutique has an entire wall devoted to tea gear—cups, pots, kettles, infusers, strainers, paper filters, little wire racks for organizing boxes, airtight jars and tins for storing loose leaf. I consider the display, tapping my lips with one finger.

Finally, I choose a squat, Japanese-style ceramic teapot with a mottled forest-green glaze. Its shelf tag reads: *Ao-Oribe ushirode kyuusu, tenmoku glaze, sasame filter.*

I haven't the faintest idea what any of that means.

And the price is slightly horrifying. But its color and elegant shape are perfect—tasteful, yet eye-catching, not too masculine or too feminine. A symbol of compromise, a hope for harmony. A gift that I chose myself, but in recognition of a ritual that Noah holds dear.

Just for the hell of it, I take a pair of matching cups too. I'll definitely stick to coffee in the mornings. But maybe, late at night, it wouldn't be so bad to share a hot cup of tea with Noah.

I make my way to the front of the store, smiling to myself, feeling calm at last.

Chapter Nine

Noah

"I'm in the mood for red meat," Sterling says as we walk down the crowded sidewalk after work.

"Damn. Dry streak, buddy?" I rub my chin thoughtfully.

"What?" He squints at me in the fading light.

"A craving for red meat usually means a lack of sex. A desire for a certain *other* kind of meat, if you will." I grin at him.

"Shut it."

Oh yeah, he's in a funk. I know for a fact he's been going through some type of dry spell, but I have no idea the cause. Before I can pry, he's chuckling next to me.

"What?" I ask.

"You're so misguided, it's not even funny. You're the one who's going to be in for the world's biggest case of blue balls—marrying someone as hot as Olivia Cane and not getting to fuck her?" He makes a pitiful noise. "That's just a damn shame."

"Who said anything about not getting to fuck her?" I pull open the door to the Grassland Steakhouse and gesture for him to enter.

He shoots me an odd glare, but approaches the hostess to request a table.

Once we're seated with our drinks—a whiskey neat for me, a pint of imported beer for him—Sterling leans closer. "Did you and your lovely bride make more headway on your relationship than I'd realized?"

I shrug. "Not yet." She's far from being my bride, for one thing. "But I, for one, am not giving up hope." I take another sip of my drink. "In fact, after dinner, I'm meeting her at our new apartment. A gift from her father."

"No shit?"

I nod.

"Living together, huh. That's a big step."

"Indeed."

For a moment, I put myself in Sterling's shoes and wonder if he's feeling like he's suddenly lost his best friend and wingman. We used to go out every weekend together hunting for pussy and fun—in that order. Now, I'm practically a married man with a new housemate, and probably a curfew.

But when I glance back at Sterling, he's grinning at me like the cat who ate the canary, and I'm certain he knows something I don't.

● ● ●

After dinner, I arrive at the penthouse first. It's a stunning apartment in the heart of the city.

I take my time looking around, flipping on light switches as I go. Expansive views from an airy twentieth-floor balcony, a modern kitchen with a little Italian coffeemaker on the counter that I'm sure Olivia will love, and expensive finishes everywhere I look— from the thick crown molding to the marble countertops to the hand-scraped oak flooring. It looks every bit like a marriage retreat. The walls and furniture, carpeting and linens are all in various shades of white and cream. It feels pure and untouched.

Honestly, it feels a bit like walking through a museum. It'll take a while to think of this place as home. I've held on to my little bachelor pad near the F Line for so long now, I don't like the idea of leaving it. But I know this is all for the best. A future with Olivia is what my father wanted for me.

And speaking of fathers . . . a bottle of red wine and two glasses have been left on the counter with a note from Olivia's dad.

Noah,

Thank you for doing this, son. I won't be around forever, and it feels so good to know that you will be there to take care of my little girl. I know you won't let me down. There's not another man I'd trust with both my company and my daughter. I hope you know that.

Very truly,

Fred Cane

I fold the paper into a square and stick it in my

pocket. I realize that Olivia's dad always trusted me with her. Even when I was a horny sixteen-year-old kid with a new driver's license, and she wasn't allowed to date, I alone was awarded the privilege of taking her on outings. We boated, played mini golf, went to the movies, you name it.

I open the bottle to let it breathe and cross the room to look out on the city skyline below. I can't help thinking back on all the good times Olivia and I have shared. And the difficult ones too. We've been there for each other through the loss of our mothers and watching our company crumble.

I stand here thinking for so long, I lose track of time. Surprised, I blink back to reality and look at my watch. *She's late.*

With a sinking feeling, I wonder if she's even coming. Why in the fuck should I care if she wants to live here or not? She's made it clear how she feels about me—how much she hates the idea of being stuck with me. I'm akin to a piece of dog shit on the bottom of her five-hundred dollar heels.

But I know there's a lot more to it than that. I'll be

sorely disappointed if she decides not to show.

Finally, there's a click in the lock. I try not to sprint to the door like a golden retriever.

Olivia comes inside. I'm not sure what I expected, but she's changed out of her work clothes and into a pair of slim-fitting jeans and a lightweight sweater.

"Hey." Leaving her suitcase by the door, she crosses the living room toward me.

"You're an hour late," I say as I make my way toward the kitchen.

"I was picking something up." She sets a brightly colored shopping bag on the counter. "Something for you, actually." She treats me to a rare, warm smile.

I watch as she removes a box from inside the shopping bag and sets it on the counter.

"Well . . . are you going to open it?" she asks.

I figured she'd want to see the apartment first, but I oblige, coming to stand beside her. I can smell the light notes of honeysuckle on her skin. Damn, that's going to be distracting if we're living together now. I'll be in a constant state of arousal. *Awesome.*

I lift open the flap on the cardboard box and dig through the packaging until I find it.

"It's a teapot," I say, holding it up and inspecting it with curiosity.

Then the meaning behind her gift slams into me. The conversation we shared about our moms comes rushing back. I don't think anyone's ever given me such a thoughtful gift before.

Olivia reaches into the shopping bag, pulls out two small cups, and sets them on the counter. "We can have tea together sometime . . . if you like."

There's a touch of uncertainty in her voice. Did she think I might not like that idea?

Well, I don't. I fucking love it.

"That was very thoughtful of you, Snowflake."

I thought my friend Sterling was the only one who got my obsession with tea, being that he's British, but apparently Olivia is on board too.

I set the teapot down on the counter and pull her in close for a hug. I expect Olivia to go rigid in my arms, or even recoil with a comment about inappropriate physical contact. But instead she's soft and warm, and her body molds to mine. Her hands rest on my shoulders and she watches me with wide eyes.

"Thank you," I say, skimming my thumb across her jaw.

"No problem."

"You know I'm going to kiss you at some point, right?"

We're so close, I can hear her swallow. The very tip of her tongue pokes out—a quick, nervous lick that she doesn't even seem aware of.

Damn, so cute . . . that's a yes if I ever saw one. But I want more than just unconscious signals. I wait to see how Olivia decides to respond.

Finally, she gives me a small nod. "Maybe," she says, trying to sound flippant.

I chuckle and release my hold on her. "Come on.

You've got to check this place out. It's incredible."

"My dad went overboard, as usual." She turns from me and gazes out at the balcony.

"Glass of wine first?"

"Why not?"

With a glass of red wine in hand, we make our way through the apartment. Olivia points out architectural details and discusses the shower schedule for the one bathroom we'll share, while I just nod along and watch her.

Being here with her, listening to her ideas for decorating, sharing this space with her . . . it feels like a start. Maybe even the start of something real.

"This isn't so bad, is it?" I tease.

She gives me a look. "Just because I nearly had a panic attack at the thought of living together doesn't mean you get to gloat."

"Fine. I won't. But it's a nice place. Your dad did well."

She nods. Then she glances away for a second. "There's something I wanted to tell you."

We start down the hall, and I motion for her to continue in front of me.

"I've taken your proposition under advisement, and here's what I propose." Olivia's tone is confident, her shoulders squared.

"My proposition?" I ask. She's being so clinical, I can't wait to hear her explain this.

She stops to look at me. "You know, that make-out idea you suggested at the bar last week. I'd be willing to try it sometime."

Hell yes. I'm finally making some real headway here.

"Sure. We could do that." *Starting as soon as humanly possible.*

"As long as there were parameters," she continues.

Parameters. Rules. Guidelines. Why am I not surprised? This woman is unlike any I've ever met before. She certainly keeps me guessing.

"Such as?"

"First base only, as I believe you said. And fully clothed." She narrows her eyes at my crotch. "Which means you keep that giant thing in your pants."

"You think I'm giant?" I can't help the smirk that uncurls on my mouth.

"Oh, for heaven's sake, stop fishing for compliments. You know it's impressive, otherwise you wouldn't have shoved it down my throat." As soon as the words leave her mouth, her face flushes bright pink, her Freudian slip sinking in.

"Oh, Snowflake." I pet her hot cheek with my thumb. "I haven't shoved it down your throat yet, but I'm very much looking forward to that."

"L-let's just forget I said that. No one will be shoving anything anywhere. First base. Got it?"

I chuckle. "I'm happy to go as slow as you need to."

And it's the truth. *Slow* may not be my usual style, but there's a certain satisfaction in knowing that I'm winning over her trust and readying her for more. The idea is quite gratifying. It will make my victory all the sweeter.

"This is going to work, me and you," I tell her as we near the bedroom.

Yes, one fucking bedroom. And before you get excited, I summon up my willpower to tell her I'll sleep on the motherfucking couch.

"You can have the bed," I say, stopping in the hallway.

It's the gentlemanly thing to do, no question. And since I did just tell her I was looking forward to putting my cock down her throat, I figure I have some making-up to do in the manners department.

"Are you sure?" Her voice is filled with surprise.

I swallow. "Of course. I'll take the couch."

Our gazes drift together from the modern, stylish tweed sofa in the living room to the massive king-sized bed down the hall dressed in fluffy down, and back to the couch again. There's no way my six-foot-two-inch frame will even fit on that couch.

"You know what?" Olivia says brightly. "We're two grown adults. It's a huge bed. We can manage sharing it, right?"

"I'll be a pussycat." I grin at her.

"That's what I'm afraid of," she murmurs.

Chapter Ten

Olivia

I let Noah take the bathroom to brush his teeth first. We haven't yet reached the level of familiarity required for me to watch another human being spit into the sink. Meanwhile, I take the bedroom to change into my favorite fleecy pajamas.

When I emerge, Noah is leaning against the wall outside the bathroom door. He cocks his head with an amused smile that stops me in my tracks.

"What?" I ask after a minute.

His eyes crinkle at the edges. "Nothing. You just look cute."

Cute? My cheeks turn pink as the word fizzes down through my stomach. I suddenly feel self-conscious about having little lavender butterflies printed all over me. Somehow I hadn't expected Noah to have an opinion on my pajamas. Or, if he did, that he would tease me about them. Not say sweet things that make me temporarily forget how to talk.

"Where are your pajamas?" I ask, shrugging off the bubbly feeling.

His smile quirks with mischief. "Well, usually I sleep in the nude—"

Of course you do. Why am I not surprised?

"Not anymore you don't," I say quickly, interrupting him. "Find some sweatpants or something." As we trade places, passing in the hallway, I add over my shoulder, "And that better include a shirt!"

The sight of Noah's sculpted six-pack while I'm still getting comfortable with the idea of sharing an apartment with him—let alone a bed? No way I'd survive that.

When I'm almost done brushing my teeth, he calls out from the bedroom. "Hey, Snowflake? Since we're spending the night together, would you be interested in taking our first test drive?"

My heart jumps into my throat. It slows down a little—but only a little—when I realize he's talking about our make-out idea. Jeez . . . give the guy an inch and he starts asking for a mile.

Surprisingly, though, I don't feel a speck of reluctance about kissing Noah. Only curiosity, a flush of warmth, a flutter of nervous excitement. But then again, our agreement is strictly limited to necking like a couple of shy high-schoolers, which we've technically already done seven years ago. And there's no reason to reevaluate my stance against casual sex—what I have planned is a long way from home base. The thought is both a huge relief and a tiny bit disappointing.

"Sure," I answer him finally, trying to sound nonchalant. I was the one who proposed we try it, after all. Although I assumed it would be a little further in the future. But tonight is as good a time as any.

At last, the moment of truth arrives. Swallowing hard, I pull back the covers, sit down, and slide underneath. The linens rustle as Noah does the same on the bed's other side.

I can hear him move and breathe. I'm attuned to every tiny sound, hyperaware of how close he is to me.

It's been so long since I slept in the same room with another person, let alone the same bed. And this is nothing like bunking with my sister or Camryn. My new bedmate is a man. A very handsome man who has made it extremely clear that he wants to fuck my brains out with his huge dick. We're only sleeping together, not *sleeping* together, but still . . . I'm sharing a bed with Noah Fucking Tate. And I'm about thirty seconds away from kissing him.

An odd fluttery energy washes over me—nervousness and excitement mix until I can't tell them apart. I feel a sudden shy urge to withdraw to my side of the bed and stare at the wall until he falls asleep, then I chide myself for being ridiculous. We're not innocent children, but we're also not teenagers, blushing and giggling at the barest mention of sex. We're two mature, liberated adults who have very sensibly decided to . . .

Another giddy wave, this one distinctly warmer. I force myself to stop being a nervous wreck and roll over.

Noah has propped himself up on his elbow. His slight smile drops as he searches my face. "Hey, are you okay?"

Are my jitters that obvious?

"Uh, y-yeah, I'm fine," I reply. Maybe that's not totally true, but it's not a lie, either. I really do want to try this. Which means I need to take the plunge now. "Let's go."

Noah nods and scoots closer. He reaches out to stroke my hair out of my face, and I relax a fraction into his light, almost tickling touch.

"Still with me?" he asks.

I nod.

"Because we don't have to do anything you don't want to."

"I know that."

His touches are more gentle than I expected. His fingertips are so light on my cheek, my neck, tucking my hair behind my ear. It's . . . nice.

Then, at last, he shifts his weight and leans in.

That first brush is so soft, I can barely feel it. It's

more like the pause before a kiss than the kiss itself. But it still kicks my heart rate into overdrive.

"Was that all right?" he murmurs, his warm and minty breath fanning over my mouth.

I tilt up my chin and answer his question with a chaste peck.

He brushes against my lips with a chuckle. Sliding one arm under my head as a pillow, he lies down facing me, draping his other arm around my shoulder and upper back. He keeps his hands high and his lower body at least an inch from mine. A gentleman . . . for now, anyway.

His mouth starts moving gently. No tongue, no teeth, not even very much pressure—just feeling the give and take of our lips against each other. My nervousness slowly drains away to be replaced with a different, much more pleasant kind of buzzing energy.

It's obvious what he's doing. He's trying to take things slow and make sure I'm comfortable. I'm relieved at his careful consideration . . . but I'm also slightly embarrassed that it was necessary in the first place. Time to up the ante a little.

I reach my arm around his waist, feeling how firm his muscles are, and open my mouth to him. With a low, quiet noise of approval, he immediately responds to my invitation. The tip of his tongue flicks over my lips. I return the move, determined to match his boldness, then let out a small gasp when he slides his tongue over mine. It's almost like I can feel that deft touch much lower. My panties are growing damp, and these stupid fleece pajamas are suddenly suffocating. His lips are so full, so soft, and his mouth moves expertly over mine.

Unbidden, my body pulls itself closer ... His skillful kisses are way better than I even remember.

And then I feel it. His half-hard length rubs against my thigh.

The thought of Noah—who starred in my every lurid teenage fantasy without my permission—hard and ready for me, now, here, in the very appealing flesh, is almost too much. A rush of heat pulses low in my belly, and I'm right on the verge of rocking my hips into him when reality strikes.

What the hell am I doing?

This is Noah Tate, who's slept with half of Manhattan, who's probably just doing this to win our bet and add another notch to his bedpost.

I freeze at the thought, and he pulls away.

"What's wrong?" he asks in confusion.

"I think it's time to stop for now," I manage to say without stumbling over my words.

His brow furrows in distinct annoyance. "Really?"

"Yes, really. Good night." I untangle myself from his embrace and roll over. "But thank you. That was fun."

"Just fun?" His tone is incredulous. "Sheesh. Leave a twenty on my nightstand while you're at it."

"Are you telling me you're familiar with that kind of situation?"

"Oh, screw you."

He rolls over and I hear him get up and walk out into the hall.

I force my eyes closed and practice deep breathing to cool down. Seriously, how have I never noticed how stifling these pajamas are?

But about fifteen minutes later, I start wondering where he went. Did he change his mind and go to sleep on the couch? I hope not . . . I'd feel guilty, even if it was his own choice. Maybe I should find him.

Sighing, I get up to check the living room. It's empty. But the bathroom door is shut, with light leaking from under it. I feel a little stupid for not guessing that in the first place. At the same time, though, it's been kind of a while. Did he fall in or something?

I walk over, raising my hand to knock on the door . . . then stop, my cheeks coloring when I hear it. An unmistakable moan of pleasure.

My eyes fly open wide. I can't believe what an idiot I am. What the hell did I think a man would do after I gave him a boner?

I should leave. Right now. I should go back to bed and pretend I didn't hear anything. So . . . why am I not moving?

A low, husky growl comes from inside the bathroom, and my breath hitches. Without meaning to, I lean closer to the door.

If I listen hard, I can hear his heavy breathing. He's loud . . . I wonder if he's getting close yet? He must be, if he's been doing this for almost fifteen minutes. Unless he has great stamina.

Another groan, this one louder and shakier. It's all too easy to imagine the scene on the other side of the bathroom door. I can't stop the mental images . . .

Noah with his sweatpants pushed down to his upper thighs and his shirt rucked up to reveal his taut abs and a dark trail of hair. His chest heaving, his legs trembling. His eyes dark and half-lidded or shut in concentration. Flushed and sweaty, his head thrown back, biting his full lips to keep quiet or parting them to gasp for breath. And his huge, hard cock—even more impressive than when I saw it in the bar a few days ago. It must be so long and thick right now, curving up proudly, swollen and veiny, the purple head wet, straining in his tight fist as he jerks himself fast and rough.

My panties flood with moisture.

He's panting harsh and loud now, each breath edged with a moan that almost sounds like half-formed words. What's he saying? What's he thinking about? I shift, rubbing my thighs together slightly.

"Olivia . . ." he groans.

My jaw drops. My pussy clenches hard on emptiness, sopping wet now. Noah calling my name like that—so ragged, so desperate—is the hottest thing I've ever heard in my life.

His noises of pleasure build to a crescendo, then taper off. Finally, he falls silent. My mouth is bone dry and I can feel my heart pounding in my throat.

Then I realize that he'll probably be coming out of the bathroom soon. And if he catches me listening at the door like some kind of Peeping Tom, he'll never let me hear the end of it.

I hustle back down the short hallway, jump into bed, and yank the covers over me just as the bathroom door opens. I slam my eyes closed. Noah's footsteps pad closer, quick and quiet. The mattress dips with a tiny creak as he gets into bed.

Lying limp, I try to keep my breathing as slow and steady as possible. Which isn't easy when I'm flooded with both lust and adrenaline. But if Noah realizes I'm feigning sleep, he doesn't act like it.

I lie there feeling like a complete idiot—my heart still hammering away, my body primed and ready— while Noah, satisfied, drifts off into a peaceful sleep.

• • •

The next morning, my alarm wakes me up to an empty bed. Strange ... I wouldn't have pegged Noah for an early bird.

Far down the hall, I can distantly hear metal clanking, and a few sniffs confirm the smell of brewing coffee. Noah must be cooking. He doesn't even drink coffee; he's made it just for me. My stomach approves of that idea. It's reassuring too—hopefully I can take it as a sign that he's not too upset about me cutting things short last night.

I roll out of bed to quickly brush my teeth, shower, and get dressed, not wanting to miss a hot breakfast.

When I walk into the kitchen, Noah is indeed standing at the stove as I thought. But I didn't predict that he'd be shirtless and still damp from the shower, his dark hair tousled, his toned muscles rippling subtly under tanned skin. I can't help but gawk a little. Show-off . . . the jerk knows exactly how good he looks.

He glances back with a smile, interrupting my horny reverie. "Sleep well?"

"Yeah, like a log," I reply as casually as possible. *Right after I lay awake for a solid hour, wetter than the goddamn Hudson River.*

Maybe I could have taken Noah's example and found my own relief, but at the time, I was too paranoid that he'd wake up and catch me. And then I'd have to put up with his swaggering for who knows how long. Eternity, most likely.

The kettle whistles, saving me from needing to say anything else other than, "I'll get that."

"Thanks." Noah speaks over his shoulder as he concentrates on the panful of hissing eggs, and my stomach growls; our food looks nearly done. "I already put the leaves in the pot."

I pour the hot water into our new teapot, fix a cup of coffee for myself, and bring everything to the table. Noah serves up two plates, each holding half of a perfect spinach-mushroom omelet.

We eat by the dining area's bay windows, enjoying the early morning's airy sunlight and the view of Manhattan sprawled out beneath us. Our conversation is surprisingly pleasant—talking shop, tossing ideas for our new business plan back and forth. I start to relax. Maybe being roommates will work fine after all. We've only stayed one night, but this place is already starting to feel like home.

I finish my last bite of eggs with a contented sigh. A fresh, hot breakfast is definitely a nice way to start my morning. My usual routine consists of grabbing a bagel or muffin while running out the door. If Noah's trying to suck up to me, it's working.

A girl could get used to this . . .

Unfortunately, we've dawdled long enough. We need to get to the office soon. I stow my plate and mug in the dishwasher and start heading to the bathroom to put on my makeup.

But as I turn, Noah catches me by the shoulders and spins me around again. His strong arms wrap tight around me. Before I can think, he crushes our lips together.

I gasp. It's nothing like last night's kiss. That was soft and sweet, the lightest possible touch, like trying not to spook a skittish animal. This is a different kind of taming—hard, rough, fiery. The kid gloves have come off. Noah has caught me, claimed me, and arousal flares through my body like the heat of a brand.

Caught off guard, I can't hold back a moan. I'm shocked to find my muscles turning to jelly. I cling to him just to stay on my feet.

Everything about Noah pours into my senses. I soak up his body heat, the rasp of stubble around my lips, the masculine scents of piney soap and spicy aftershave.

He devours my mouth and leaves me dizzy, panting for air. His teeth nip and scrape at my lips. His tongue licks deep, skating over mine, a tantalizing preview of how that hot, agile muscle might move over my clit. A vivid promise of the pleasure I could have . . . if I'd only let him give it to me.

I remember how he moaned my name in the bathroom last night. The memory of those dark, needy noises send another flood of heat through me. Maybe I'm not just another conquest to him; maybe he's just as powerless in his own way.

Suddenly, I can't figure out why I ever hesitated. I had a hot, willing man practically begging to blow my mind. What was the point of denying myself a good time? I arch up, pressing our hips together, and feel a twin flash of hunger and triumph at the long, thick hardness that pokes into my belly.

Then Noah steps back. All the touch I'm craving— the warm, muscled body and the hot, wet mouth— suddenly just disappears. It takes me a moment to register what happened.

Still dazed with lust, I blink up at him. "What . . . ?"

"It's time to leave. We're going to be late for

work."

"Work?" The word comes out as a disappointed whine.

He grins like he just won the Super Bowl. "You're the one who set our limits at first base. Although, if you want more, I think the office could survive another hour without us. But you'll have to ask nicely."

As the fog of horniness clears away from my mind, I realize what's going on here. *Oh, you son of a bitch . . .*

Noah was playing with me this whole time. His plan all along was to tease me until I got desperate enough to loosen our agreement's restrictions. He's trying to tempt me into admitting that I want to be more than just friends. He thinks he can prove himself right and also get laid—two birds with one stone.

Well, he can just forget about it. Olivia Cane does not beg. Ever.

I'm almost more pissed off at myself than him. What the hell was I thinking? Not much, that's for sure. My libido just totally ripped me out of the driver's seat. I've never felt so out of control before. And if I have anything to say about it, this first time will also be the last.

Damn, my lips still tingle from his kiss. My face burns with embarrassment and the last stubborn traces of arousal.

Trying to collect myself, I give Noah the dirtiest look I can muster. "You're the devil."

"I'm pretty sure that would make you the queen of hell, then." He pauses. "Actually, maybe that's not so inaccurate . . ."

"Congratulations, smartass, you get to finish the dishes while I put on my makeup." I turn on my heel and stalk away to the bathroom.

"As you wish," he calls down the hall after me.

I set my jaw, trying to tamp down my irritation and lingering horniness. I know of only one sure way to shut him up. Unfortunately, as I just learned, he would only turn a kiss to his advantage again.

I can't forget Noah's boast about how I'd be begging by Day Four. At first, I thought there was no

way I'd give in that easily. But now, only one-day later,
I'm not so sure.

Chapter Eleven

Noah

When we reach the conference room, it's filled to capacity with nearly all the office staff in the building. All the seats at the long conference table are taken, and it's standing room only at the back of the room.

I see Rosita tucked into the far corner and she gives me a cheerful wave. She wasn't on the invite for the meeting, but I texted her to be here. There's no way I could let her miss out on hearing the big news. I know she's as proud of me as my own mother would have been.

Olivia's father is standing at the head of the room, chatting casually with Prescott and the few members of the board who opted to show. I know they're less than optimistic about the results Olivia and I are promising.

As we wait for the big announcement to begin, people are talking in small groups. Some chat about the work they're so passionate about, while others are just making small talk with the workplace friends they've developed over the years. These are all the people who'll lose their jobs if we're not successful. Real people. With real problems and real lives. And all of that is on the line.

My stomach tightens.

"I need a drink," Olivia grumbles beside me.

"Good idea," I murmur.

I wonder if she's still pissed at me for leaving her high and dry this morning. Probably. But after the way she rolled her tight little ass over in bed last night after giving me a hard-on with her soft, wet kisses and little groans of encouragement? Forcing me to go tend to the beast if I wanted any hope of falling asleep? Yeah, payback's a bitch.

Her gaze wanders to the side table near the windows, where carafes of coffee and trays of Danishes have been placed.

"I don't see any tea. You want coffee?" she asks, already starting toward it.

I shake my head. "Thanks for asking, but I'm

good."

Moments later, Olivia returns with a paper cup of steaming black coffee.

"Let's begin," Fred announces in a booming voice. Silence settles over the room, and all eyes focus on him.

He takes a step forward. "I've called this meeting today to share a special announcement." He looks over at me and Olivia and smiles briefly before turning his attention back out onto the crowd. "It is with great honor that I announce the next generation of Tate & Cane . . . my daughter, Olivia, and Bill's son, Noah, are taking over operations as co-CEOs."

A murmur of whispers erupts all around us.

"I know, I know." Fred silences the crowd with a wave of his hand. "The family decided to reject the board's proposal, at least for now, and prove to you that we can turn this company profitable under their leadership by the end of this financial quarter."

We see a few heads nodding, but most people still look uncertain. I don't blame them. Their jobs are at stake, and what proof do they have that Olivia and I can actually pull this off—and so fast? None.

"Please put your hands together and welcome your new co-CEOs." He claps enthusiastically and everyone follows suit, treating us to a round of applause.

After the noise dies down, Olivia steps forward with a short but eloquent speech about how devoted we are to succeeding, and how we'll need the cooperation and hard work of everyone in this room to win together. Honestly, I'm not sure exactly what she says because I see Harrison eye-fucking Olivia from where he stands in the back of the room, and blood thunders in my ears.

As Olivia finishes, I step forward and take her hand in mine. That prick from accounting is about to know for certain who she belongs to.

"I have a related announcement, actually. Might as well get it all out in the open, since I have nothing to hide." I grin at Olivia, who looks like she's ready to murder me. "The rumors are true. Olivia and I are dating."

"But it won't detract from our business focus," she says, interrupting me.

Damn. Everything about this woman is stiff and unrelenting. What I need is to get her to loosen up and relax. She's wound too tight. She needs to learn to stop and smell the roses once in a while. Work aside, that becomes my next priority.

Plus, I still have to figure out how I'm going to win the bet we've made. Only three more days to get her wet and naked and begging for me . . . And just like that, it moves up to the top of my agenda.

I fight off the wave of arousal that hits me and smile as we field questions from the employees.

• • •

As soon as the meeting ends and the entire company isn't watching us, Olivia storms away without a word and refuses to answer my knock on her office door. I guess my little impromptu announcement pissed her off even more than I thought.

But why? We *are* dating, aren't we? Damn it . . . if I ever want to win her over, I need to figure out what makes her tick. I'm not above asking for help. And who knows a woman better than her best friend?

I already know Camryn works in the marketing department. Tracking down her cubicle is easy from there. When I find it, I see it's a mess of papers and folders, one of those chaotic systems where I'm sure she'd try to convince me she knows where everything is.

She's typing away, and when I stroll up, her fingers suddenly stop and her eyes lift to mine.

"How can I help you?"

I almost laugh. She's so formal. She and Olivia are definitely cut from the same cloth; I can see why they're such good friends.

"I need to talk to you about Olivia," I say, and Camryn's brow furrows.

It crosses my mind that maybe she won't want to help me. I decide to lay all my cards on the table and see if my candor will make her bite.

I lower my voice and lean in closer. "You know about the whole marriage contract, right?"

"Yes, and I'm not going to help you try to convince her, if that's why you're here. Olivia's a big girl, and she can make up her own mind."

"That's not why I'm here."

"Fine. What do you need? I'm not exactly *Team Noah*, you know?"

"That's fine, because we're both Team Olivia."

She swivels her chair away from the keyboard and faces me. "You have five minutes."

"Why is Olivia so opposed to this? I hate to be so cocksure, but most women drop their panties at my slightest interest."

"Olivia is *not* most women."

"Believe me, I've noticed."

"So, what seems to be the problem, lover boy?" She shifts her weight in her seat, looking me over with an amused expression. She's enjoying my desperation way too much. "I never imagined that Noah Tate, the legendary sex god, would have any problem seducing a woman."

"Sex god, eh?"

She shrugs. "Are the rumors true or not?"

"Depends on which rumors you're referring to."

"That you have a magical nine-inch dick that tastes like strawberries?"

I burst out laughing despite myself. We're in a crowded work area with people sitting well within earshot, and she's discussing my cock like we're picking out carpet samples.

"As much as it pains me to say this, let's get off my dick and onto the topic at hand."

She squares her shoulders. "Right. Olivia."

"Tell me what she likes. Hobbies. Interests. Things she enjoys."

Camryn takes a second to think it over. "She works her ass off all week, which I'm sure you know. So if you're referring to the weekends, she likes watching rom-coms and has a secret romantic side. She buys herself a bouquet of peonies at the farmers' market every Saturday."

"That's good." I pull out my phone and type *peonies*

into the notes app. "What else? Favorite color? Food?" I already know she likes dirty martinis and red wine, but charming Olivia will take a lot more than just liquoring her up.

"Green. Like money." Camryn grins. Olivia always was an overachieving powerhouse. "And she loves tapas."

"Isn't that just appetizers for dinner?"

"Basically," Camryn says with a shrug.

"Got it. Anything else?"

She looks away for a moment. "Well, there is one thing, but I don't think you're going to want to hear this."

"Lay it on me."

"She has this scrapbook of her dream wedding. She's been adding to it since she was a little girl."

"Olivia?" My eyes widen. "The same Olivia Cane who protested getting married has dreams of a grand wedding?"

"Exactly. She's always dreamed of a big, beautiful wedding. She's actually really mushy underneath that hard shell. What her mom and dad shared was special, and she's ultimately looking for the same thing. The perfect wedding. The perfect husband."

It all hits me at once. "And this arrangement crushes her lifelong dream."

"Well, yes."

Camryn seems oblivious of the huge bombshell she just dropped on me. It doesn't matter if I know Olivia's favorite color or dinner spot. She wants the one thing I can never give her—a real happily-ever-after.

My heart sinks a little. No matter how well we're getting along, I'm not foolish enough to think I could fill in for her soul mate. *Unless* . . . I swallow as a wave of nerves hits. Holy freaking matrimony. Am I ready for that?

"One more thing," I ask Camryn. "Why doesn't she ever date?" Not since that douche of an ex in college have I seen Olivia with another man.

"Basically? She's a picky bitch," Camryn says with a

fond smile.

"She's waiting for her Prince Charming to sweep her off her feet."

"Something like that."

"Thanks, this has been really helpful."

"Good luck," Camryn calls as I head toward my office. She lets the *you're going to need it* go unspoken.

Fuck . . . I've got my work cut out for me.

Chapter Twelve

Olivia

On Noah's tuxedo-clad arm, I walk into Clair de Lune, a five-star French restaurant overlooking the East River. Escargot, caviar, white tablecloths, hundred-dollar bottles, the whole nine yards.

Even though this event is purely business—a dinner meeting meant to win over a new client—Noah brought me a bouquet of peonies when he came to my office to pick me up. He was polite and attentive, and it almost made me forgive him for getting me riled up the other day.

Who am I kidding? The man riles me up every five minutes.

The hostess guides us to our reserved table, where Miss Estelle Osbourne, the forty-something chief marketing officer of Parrish Footwear, is already seated with a glass of champagne in front of her. She looks regal in her lavender-gray chiffon evening gown, its sheer capped sleeves appliqued with silver lace—a sexy, yet sophisticated touch. I suddenly feel both underdressed and frumpy in my simple knee-length black sheath.

I read Miss Osbourne's business profile online while studying up on her company for this dinner. After completing her Ivy League education, she landed a job with fashion giant Luxor Brands and has been climbing the corporate ladder ever since. She just took over Parrish's esteemed head of marketing role last year, and so far she's doing great things.

Talented, successful, beautiful, with keen business instincts . . . she's exactly the kind of woman I strive to be. Which only makes the prospect of trying to impress her more nerve-racking.

"She got here early? Now it looks like we're late," I hiss under my breath.

"Relax, Snowflake," Noah murmurs as he pulls out my chair for me.

Easy for him to say. How does he always stay so cool? I'm balanced on a knife's edge of excitement and anxiety. Getting hold of this new client in the first place was an unbelievable stroke of good fortune. If we manage to charm this woman, her company's contracts will go a long way toward digging us out of the red. Tate & Cane desperately needs this business dinner to come off without a hitch.

After everyone shakes hands and introduces themselves, Noah and I sit down. The waiter materializes with the wine list and three menus. I order the beef bourguignon and a glass of last year's Beaujolais nouveau. *Bring on the red wine.*

The waiter departs and I take a sip of ice water to clear my dry throat. *Don't worry, you've got this.*

"So, as I was saying earlier on the phone, Tate & Cane is currently implementing a solid plan for—"

"Oh, surely business can wait until after the main course." Miss Osbourne, or Estelle, as she's told us to call her, interrupts with a smile that says she's clearly accustomed to getting her way. "How long have you two been together?"

"Uh . . ."

How the hell do I explain that we're in the trial phase of an arranged marriage? We only started dating a few days ago, but in a sense, we're sort of . . . pre-engaged? I should probably just make something up. And I have to do it fast because I've already paused for way too long. But I also have to make sure my lie won't come back to bite us in the ass later.

"For as long as we can remember," Noah says, smoothly covering the awkward silence. "Our fathers were close friends and business partners, so we spent most of our childhoods together. It was meant to be."

"How sweet." Estelle simpers, looking between us with curiosity.

"In fact, that reminds me of a story from when our families summered together . . ."

Oh God, here it comes. Noah deploys one of his secret weapons: a cute anecdote about how he once saved a puppy from drowning in Shinnecock Bay. It's an old tale, wildly embellished over the years, guaranteed to make women fawn and panties disintegrate.

I start tuning it out in favor of concentrating on the

fragrant food that just arrived. I'll let Noah have his playtime for now. It's probably a decent strategy to let our prospective client get a few drinks deep before pitching our business anyway.

Eventually, Noah finishes his story amid Estelle's approving murmurs. I start listening again when he leans slightly toward her, his manner conspiratorial, as if he's about to say something intimate and profound. But all he asks is, "Tell me . . . would you happen to be named after Estelle Carmen, the Hollywood designer?"

Estelle actually giggles. "You and I both know I'm too old for that to be true. She was only a girl when I was born. But I appreciate the attempt at flattery."

"Really? I would have sworn otherwise." He flashes her a thousand-watt grin.

"Stop it," she says in a coy lilt that tells him to do no such thing. "But I'm surprised you know that name at all. Are you a student of fashion, Mr. Tate?"

"I'm always interested in what beautiful women are wearing . . . or not."

"You ought to be more careful with that fresh

mouth of yours," she says, scolding him playfully.

What the hell is happening here? Did I suddenly turn invisible to them?

I shoot a glance at our waiter, who's cleared the main course dishes and asked twice if we'd like dessert. He looks almost as irritated as I feel, which is both reassuring and terrifying.

At least I know I'm not just going crazy here, but I hate that Noah and Estelle's antics are so visible. With the way they're carrying on, anyone would assume they were old friends ... or maybe even a couple. I'm the odd man out. My only companions are an empty wineglass and the first hints of an oncoming headache.

"Sorry about that," I tell the waiter. "Yes, please go ahead and bring us the dessert menu. And the cocktail menu too. Thank you." *Gotta buy time to get this dinner back on track ...*

I seriously have no idea what's going on. Noah and I reviewed our game plan at the office just a few hours ago—talk numbers, explain why Estelle should trust her company's advertising campaigns to Tate & Cane, and get a commitment, even an informal one. But he's gone totally off script.

They've covered a wide range of topics from their favorite sushi bar (they share the same one), to the best Vegas hotels, to last year's dip in the stock market—which Parrish Footwear weathered quite well, thanks to Estelle's forward thinking—but nothing to do with securing her business. No hard facts, no persuasive arguments, no recognition of the entire fucking reason we came here tonight.

So far, I haven't managed to get out a single sentence of the sales pitch I spent three hours preparing. Not to mention that the way he's flirting with her makes me want to puke. Aren't we supposed to be boyfriend and girlfriend? Because Noah sure as hell hasn't been playing the part.

We can't walk away tonight until we have a firm idea of whether or not Parrish is with us, which means I have a long damn way to go. And the first thing I need to do is have a word with my dear sweet boyfriend. Preferably someplace private, where our client can't hear me ripping his balls off.

I check my phone, pretending that I heard it ding, then interrupt their lovefest with a plastered-on smile. "Honey, can I steal you away for a moment? My father just texted me with an important question."

Without waiting for a response, I push out my chair and stand up, grabbing Noah's hand. I drag him all the way to the back of the restaurant, near the kitchen's swinging doors. A passing waiter gives us a curious look.

"What the fuck do you think you're doing?" I growl, trying to keep my voice low despite burning with rage.

Noah blinks in surprise. Then a smug grin begins to dawn over his face. "Don't tell me you're jealous of me paying attention to another woman. That's so cute. Don't worry, Snowflake. You're the only girl I have eyes for."

I correct him with barely restrained fury. "Don't you dare try to flirt your way out of this one, you self-obsessed ass. I couldn't give a damn about where your eyes go. I'm pissed because you're making our relationship look like a joke, and I don't appreciate being the punch line. You were practically licking the béarnaise sauce off her fingers!"

Another waiter passes by. This one looks amused. I don't really blame him—we must look ridiculous, a pair of socialites dressed to the nines and feuding outside the kitchen.

I grind my teeth. I'm already humiliated and mad enough that everything just makes me feel worse.

Noah scoffs at me. "Oh, come on. It's called networking. Greasing the wheels. She knows it's nothing serious. I've done this kind of thing a million times."

Why am I not surprised? "That hardly makes me feel better. And our waiter seemed confused as to who the couple was here, me and you or you and her."

"Who gives a shit what he thinks? She's the one holding the purse strings. She's who we're here to impress."

"I'm asking you to give a shit what *I* think!"

He blinks. "What? Of course I—"

"No, you clearly don't, because otherwise you'd be listening good and hard right now."

He throws up his hands. "Okay, fine. I'm listening. Just explain what the problem is."

I suck in a deep breath through my nose, trying to calm down enough to put my thoughts in order. "Let me spell it out for you. You're the one who made such a big deal about putting on a good performance, keeping up appearances, making our relationship look real. And now you're acting like the same manwhore you've always been. Except now, I'm here to catch your collateral damage, and it's embarrassing. You *disrespected* me."

His eyes shoot open wide. "I never meant—"

"It doesn't matter! Your intent doesn't change the results. Maybe it never even occurred to you that I'd have a problem with your bullshit. I can give you that benefit of the doubt. But I'm standing here now, telling you how I feel. So, please knock it off."

He covers his mouth with one hand, pulling down hard, and lets out a loud, harried sigh. "I . . . didn't look at it like that. I was just trying to woo the client. Like I always do."

Wow, he actually looks taken aback.

Somewhat shocked, I let my voice soften. "Well, if I'm in your life now, that can't happen anymore."

"In my life, huh?" He considers me with an expression I can't quite read. "So that goes both ways, I guess. I'm in your life too?"

"Seems that way." I sigh. "We're stuck together for a good long while, at least."

Now I can read his face—the first flickers of that familiar sinful smile. He reaches up, and at first I think it's to cup my chin. But then he just runs his finger down my neck, that long stretch of exposed skin, all the way over the curve of my shoulder. I can't help my shiver.

"You make it sound like a jail sentence," he teases.

I smile. Only slightly, but it's there.

He leans even closer and asks, "Are you sure you weren't jealous at all?"

My two glasses of wine have lowered my guard. That's my excuse for why, instead of telling him to shut up, I admit, "Maybe a tiny bit." Then I regain my senses and add, "But that doesn't change my original point."

He raises his eyebrows but doesn't say anything.

My cheeks start to warm as he regards me. Why did the jerk even ask, if he was just going to stand there staring?

"What?" I'm starting to get embarrassed again, but it's different from before—a ticklish, almost excited twist in my stomach, instead of an upset, painful tightening. And the defensive tone of my own voice only intensifies the feeling.

"Nothing. I'm just a little surprised, that's all."

I roll my eyes in an attempt to stop staring into his. "Come on, don't give me that. You know the effect you have on women."

That grin is full-blown now. "Why don't you tell me?"

"No. I refuse to play travel agent for your ego trip."

"If you want, I can take my turn first." Before I can

stop him, Noah starts listing my pros. "You're the smartest, most diligent person I've ever met. Watching you work is fucking hot—in your element, poised and confident, the way your pretty blue eyes flash when you're about to tear some poor schmuck apart. I can't help wondering if you're just as fierce and tireless and creative in bed. You're honest to a fault . . . is your body honest too? Do you wear pleasure on your sleeve? Or would you try to hold back, make me work for it? Believe me, I'm up to the challenge."

His words knock me breathless. What the hell just happened? And why does it have to make me tingle in the worst way?

The half praise, half dirty talk strikes a weak point I didn't even know I had. Or maybe I only feel this way because it's Noah who's saying such sweet, filthy things, gazing at me so fervently. His husky voice softens and warms me, and I suddenly feel so exposed. Unshielded. But not in a bad way, not like a naked-at-the-important-meeting nightmare, because I know that Noah would never hurt me. He would never take advantage of my vulnerability.

Or maybe he would, but only in the ways that I secretly want.

Noah takes my hands, turns my palms up in surrender, his thumbs rubbing light circles onto the soft thin skin under my wrists. When I can't repress the shiver that races through me, he grins like a wolf. Oh, he saw that reaction, all right. He knows exactly what he's doing, and I both hate it and love it.

"And I'd do just about anything to get my hands on your amazing body," he continues mercilessly. "I've never seen a more perfect woman . . . every inch of you, tight ass and luscious tits and legs just made to wrap around my back. Kissing you the other night wasn't nearly enough. I'd love to watch your expression change as I pound into you. Watch you give up control, turn off your brain and just feel."

"Y-you don't play fair," I finally manage to stutter.

"Hey, that's not how this works. Compliments, not insults. Believe me, I already have a pretty good idea of what you think my bad points are."

"Uh . . ." I swallow. "You're pretty cool too, but in

a different way. Good with people and words and stuff, instead of numbers and strategy."

"Is that why you're blushing right now?"

In a way, yes. But his sculpted jaw, full lips, and piercing dark eyes are what make his words truly intoxicating. And the fact that he still hasn't let go of my hands.

"You take charge, and sometimes I hate that, but sometimes . . . it's nice to have a break."

His smile turns mischievous. "Oh? I'll be sure to make a note of that. Anything else?"

I retreat to safe, familiar ground. Harsh words, something I can deny later as *just a joke.* "Are you just trying to get me to admit you have a nice ass?"

But when his only response is a silky, dark chuckle, I realize my mistake. He wasn't fooled at all—*why did I ever think he would be?*—and now I've backed myself into a corner. Literally and figuratively. As I talked, Noah slowly leaned closer, bit by bit, until I can just barely feel the tickle of his breath.

Suddenly, acutely aware of the rising temperature between us, I cut myself off. "Shouldn't we get back? It's rude to keep Miss Osbourne waiting."

Noah's stare is too intense for me to look away. "The only woman I'm interested in entertaining right now is you."

I shift a fraction, needing to leave but wanting to stay, and I realize that my panties are soaking wet. Everything I never let myself feel or think about Noah rushes to the surface. My body doesn't care that he's a juvenile jerk. I hate that my libido is so totally out of my control. I hate that I've always had such a wicked crush on Noah. *Fate must be laughing her ass off at me right now.*

Noah leans even closer, stopping just short of contact. I can almost feel the brush of his lips against mine, and my stomach clenches with desire.

"Still only first base?" he whispers against my skin. "Or do you want more?"

I don't answer. I'm not even sure I can speak. I just wet my lips.

That one tiny move is like loosening a coiled

spring. Noah lunges forward to devour my mouth. My knees weaken with his expert onslaught. His strong arms wrap around me and his hands are everywhere, igniting my nerves, fingertips grazing what feels like every inch of bare skin. I feel a flash of frustration that my dress is so modest; I want his touch all over me, unrestrained.

He yanks our hips together and I feel his erection press into my belly. Something wild shoots through me, a fierce, territorial satisfaction. That hardness is all for me. Not Estelle, not any of his past conquests. I'm the one who's making him feel this way right now. Such powerful, primal need aimed squarely at me and only me.

He's all mine. The unbidden thought strikes deep into an animal part of me I never realized I had.

On fire, I cup his bulge through his pants, wanting to assert control and show off my sexual power. But that was a big mistake . . . emphasis on *big*. Feeling just how impressive and steely hard he is only makes me even more desperate. I groan and squeeze him in my palm.

"If you don't stop, we're going to have a problem," he growls out.

I giggle, feeling almost tipsy with lust. "You sure it's *our* problem and not just yours?"

He abruptly draws back, pulling an involuntary noise of disappointment from my throat. But my fervor spikes again when he takes my hand and hurries me toward the nearby restroom. He pulls me inside and locks the door. I drop my purse in the corner just as he shoves me up against the wall.

Our mouths crash together again, lips and tongue moving like they were made for this. Our making out intensifies as his fingers fumble at the back of my dress. He finds the zipper, tugs it halfway down, then abandons it to push my sleeves down past my shoulders, trapping my upper arms.

I squeal in shock—then quickly clap my hand over my mouth—when he kneels to swirl his tongue around one nipple and pinch the other . . . hard.

"No bra tonight?" he murmurs between licks and suckles and gentle bites. "Naughty girl."

I want to explain that this dress doesn't work with a bra. I want to tell him to shut up and fuck me. But all I can do is tremble at the sparks of sensation shooting from my breasts straight to my clit.

"God, these are beautiful," he says on a groan, taking my nipple in his mouth.

I can only watch, desperate, as he kisses my breasts, and let out helpless moans.

"And so sensitive." He moves to the other, giving it a wet kiss that ends with an audible sucking sound. He hikes up my skirt and runs his fingers along the center of my panties. "Just as I thought," he murmurs. "Nice and wet for me."

I open my mouth to argue, but Noah chooses that moment to kiss me again.

Then he lifts the side of my panties and his fingers slide in. No fumbling at all now, no fooling around, no teasing—he knows exactly what I'm dying for. One long finger parts me, petting me, putting just the right amount of pressure on that swollen bud. I mumble some unintelligible groan. Noah's tongue continues working against mine. Then two deft fingers crook deep inside me and the heel of his hand rubs my aching, swollen clit. Heat surges through my core and I choke out a cry of relief. *Yes . . .*

Noah growls with possessive satisfaction. "That's what I like to hear, baby. This pussy is mine now, and we both know it. I'm going to take damn good care of my *wife . . .*"

His dirty talk pisses me off and sets my body on fire all at the same time. I don't know what to feel. I can't think at all. I just hang on to Noah, struggling to keep standing while the white-hot pleasure coils tighter and tighter. I bite my lip hard to muffle my moans.

"Fuck . . . Noah . . ." I moan, rolling my hips hard against his hand. I'm so agonizingly close. Just a few more seconds . . .

Someone knocks at the door.

We both freeze in place, me topless and clutching Noah's shoulders, Noah with his hand up my skirt. The absurdity of the picture suddenly strikes me. I might have laughed if I weren't so terror-stricken—and teetering on the edge of a mind-blowing climax. Even with the fear of getting caught washing ice through my veins, I'm still burning up.

"If you move your fingers, I'll kill you," I whisper frantically to Noah. No way would I be able to keep this orgasm quiet. It's been six long months in the making. And I want it more than I want my next breath.

"Hello? Is anyone in there?"

Oh my God. That's Estelle's voice. Our client is standing less than three feet away, and my stupid sexy boyfriend's hand is *still down my panties*.

"It's Noah and Olivia," Noah calls, pulling off a perfect casual voice. "We just had a few things to talk about."

"In the bathroom?" she asks with obvious skepticism.

Is she suspicious or just confused? Damn it, I should just throw myself out the window right now.

"Private family matters, you understand. We'll just be another minute."

After a heart-stopping pause, I finally hear her footsteps move away.

"Stop touching me," I hiss under my breath.

Noah gives me a *hey, not fair* look. "You told me not to move my—"

"You know what I meant, smartass! Now get out of my panties!"

Chuckling, he withdraws. "I think that's the first time a woman's ever said that to me."

"If you want to hear worse, that can be arranged. Now, zip me up."

After Noah helps me yank my clothes back into place, I check the mirror over the sink. Jesus, I look like a train wreck. Lipstick smeared everywhere, hair rumpled. My appearance practically screams *I just humped a guy in the bathroom!* What a great bargain ... all the public embarrassment of sex with none of the "actually getting to have an orgasm" part.

I retrieve my purse from the corner, pull my travel brush through my hair a few times, then start scrubbing at my lips. As I apply a fresh coat of lipstick, I notice that Noah hasn't moved from his spot. He's straightened his tie and rebuttoned his jacket, but other than that, he's just been waiting patiently for me.

He could at least have the decency to look ashamed about tempting me into this mess . . .

"Aren't you going to wash your hands?" I snap at him. One of them was just buried in my you-know-what, after all.

With a wicked grin, he lifts that hand to his nose and makes a show of smelling his fingers, inhaling my scent, and my face flares bright red.

"No way," he says simply.

I tear my hungry eyes away and huff, "Whatever. Let's just get back to the table and hope we haven't already ruined this deal."

"Uh, sweetheart . . ."

I glance back at him. "What?"

He releases a deep breath slowly through his nose. "If I go back out there like this, I'll be arrested for indecency."

I follow his gaze, which has dropped to the front of his slacks.

Holy hell. It looks like he's smuggling a pineapple in his underwear.

"Get that thing under control."

He squeezes his eyes closed and takes another deep breath. When his eyes open again, he looks slightly more composed. "Let's roll."

As we leave the bathroom, I try to pull myself together. With Estelle in my sights again, I get my head back in work mode.

Sure, Noah may be unfairly attractive—and now I know he's good with his hands too, on top of being a skilled kisser—but I still need to stay frosty here. He's an arrogant, cocky, immature playboy who doesn't take business seriously enough.

So, keep your head in the game, Olivia, I remind myself.

But the unsatisfied ache between my thighs is almost too much to bear. This dinner will definitely qualify as the longest evening of my life.

Chapter Thirteen

Noah

"Well, that went well," I say as I maneuver my sleek black Tesla out of the parking garage. I give the gas pedal a modest tap and we fly off down the street.

I feel ten feet tall, as smug as can be, and I don't give a shit right now. Not even the way my cock is aching like a motherfucker can ruin my mood.

Olivia shoots me a questioning glare, and I know she's wondering what I'm referring to—the business meeting with the new client that we'll probably land, or my favorite part, almost getting her off in the bathroom. My body is still primed and ready to deliver.

"I can't believe you didn't wash your hands," she snaps.

"I may never wash this hand again." I smile and make a lewd gesture with my fingers.

She turns away from me with a huff and looks out her window in silence the rest of the way home.

When we arrive, the penthouse is dark and quiet and my hormones are still raging. Olivia sets her purse and cell phone down on the entry table, then turns, putting her back toward me.

"Will you unzip me?"

I drag her zipper down her back, letting my fingers graze her skin, appreciating the twin dimples in the small of her back and the very top of her lacy thong.

Torture. This is pure torture.

Taking a chance, I lean forward and place a soft kiss against the back of her neck. "We could finish what we started at the restaurant."

Her breathing has grown shallow and I can practically smell her arousal. I know her panties are still soaked. The idea of touching her again has me nearly overcome with desire.

"It's probably not a good idea. We should keep this strictly professional from now on. We need to focus on the business, don't you think?"

But she sounds the slightest bit unsure, and that's

all I need. It tells me that it's only a matter of time until I get what I want. And what I want is her tight cunt wrapped around my cock, where I can pound away for hours. Days, even.

"You were so close back there. I could feel your pussy gripping my fingers, that swollen little clit pulsing in time with every heartbeat. You were about to come," I whisper.

The heat of my breath sends a rash of goose bumps racing down the back of her neck. I know a woman's body well, how to read all the signs and signals, and everything about Olivia is blaring that she needs to be fucked. Stripped down, laid on the bed, and worshiped like the goddess she is.

"Noah . . ." Her voice is almost a groan, and my cock hardens instantly.

"What do you do for fun, Snowflake? Everything can't be about work. Sometimes blowing off some steam is a good thing."

"For everything there is a season." She straightens her posture. "And this is our season to buckle down and focus on business, not play grab-ass games. I'm sure that's a foreign concept to you, but—"

"Believe me, I'm dead serious about Tate & Cane. But business is for the workday. After hours is for playtime. And in case you failed to notice . . ." I trail one fingertip down her spine, lingering at the waistband to her panties. "It's dark outside. And we're two consenting adults."

"Two? Try counting again."

The ice princess takes a step away from me and heads toward the bedroom, where I drink in one last glimpse of her bared back and hips before she shuts the door. I can just imagine her letting the dress slip down her long legs, the fabric pooling around her still-heeled feet, her firm ass covered only with a scrap of lace . . .

God. Fucking. Damn it.

I rake my fingers through my hair and blow out a frustrated sigh. For a second, I don't know if I'm frustrated because I'm horny and insanely attracted to her, or because she's making it impossible to win our bet.

No. Fuck that. It's just because I want her. I want to take her in my arms and understand that we could really have something here. She's just so damn stubborn. And her secret dream of a romantic wedding—I may not be her first pick, but I want to at least meet her halfway, as more than friends. I'll just have to find a way to pull this off and keep everyone happy.

For now, I go into the bathroom and close the door behind me. I don't lock it . . . just in case there's a sliver of a chance Olivia changes her mind. I undo my belt and tug down my dress pants just enough to free my aching cock. Then I squirt some of her scented lotion into my palm and begin to stroke myself.

Her light, feminine scent surrounds me, and the sensations tingling along my spine mean this won't take long. For the second time this week, I work my big hand up and down my cock, wishing it were her small, delicate hand instead.

Memories of tonight in the restaurant restroom flash through my mind like an erotic dream. God, she was so ready after just a few minutes of banter and kissing. Her rosy nipples were tightened into little buds, and when I sucked and licked, they pebbled against my tongue. She tasted so sweet and made the best little grunting whimpers I've ever heard.

And then when I slipped my fingers into her panties—I half expected her to tell me to stop, only she didn't. Instead, she stepped her heeled feet further apart. The tiniest possible movement, but I was so attuned to her, I noticed. She *wanted* me to touch her. Craved it just as badly as I did. She was warm and wet, sweet, silky perfection. And when I slipped two fingers inside, I almost came right then. Her cunt was so tight, it gripped my fingers and sucked at them, greedy for me to fuck her.

I shudder at the memory. So perfect. Beautiful. Intelligent. Sexual. She's the total package.

A few more long pulls and I come hard with a grunt.

• • •

"Are you sure about this?" Olivia asks.

Her gaze wanders over to the couple dozen

partygoers scattered across Rosita's lawn. People are laughing and chatting in small groups, and upbeat Mexican pop plays from a boom box on the patio. The chain-link fence separates her yard from an auto shop behind her house. A single tree stands tall in the center with a festive piñata hanging from a branch.

"Of course. This is going to be great. Come on." I tug her toward Rosita and the birthday girl, Maria.

I drop down to one knee in front of her. "Wow. Thirty-six today, huh?"

She shakes her head, her braided pigtails bobbing wildly. "No. I'm seven!" she boasts.

"Ah, seven. Well, happy birthday." I give her a wink and she wrinkles her nose. She's definitely still at the age where boys are gross. "That's a very pretty dress you have on today."

She looks down at her hot-pink dress with decorative tangerine stitching. "Thank you. My mommy made it." She smiles up at Rosita.

When I rise to my feet, I give Rosita a hug. "Everything looks great. Thank you for inviting us."

"Of course, *mi amor*. Thank you for coming," she says to both me and Olivia. It was a one-hour drive to Jersey, but well worth it.

"Of course," Olivia echoes, her smile only a little guarded. She's obviously out of her element here, but trying her best to cope.

"Please, enjoy yourselves. There's plenty to eat, and drinks are inside."

I survey the picnic table that's so overloaded, not an inch of tabletop is showing. Empanadas, carne asada, arroz con pollo, a bunch of things I don't recognize but am game to try, and a beautiful tres leches cake in the center of it all.

"You made enough to feed an army," I say with a chuckle.

"My family has big appetites." Rosita grins wryly at me.

I hand my gift bag to Rosita. It has a couple of Spanish chapter books for Maria. I know that keeping her family's culture alive and ensuring her kids are bilingual is important to Rosita. It's something she and I have talked about before, and I think it's damn smart. Anyone who knows two languages will have a leg up in the business world when the time comes.

"Oh, you didn't have to bring a gift. Your presence here is enough."

I shake my head. "Of course I brought a gift. What birthday party is complete without a big pile of presents?"

Rosita's smile falls slightly. "Things are a little tight right now. I made Maria's gifts myself this year."

Oh shit. I meant to make a playful idle comment, not call attention to the small gift pile.

"Is everything okay?"

Rosita nods. "With all the uncertainty at work right now, I'm trying to stretch our budget and put something away for savings. Just in case."

Her gaze darts between Olivia and me as if she's looking for answers. With her having six kids, I know her budget didn't have much wiggle room to begin with.

I take Rosita's hands in mine and give them a

squeeze. "Everything will be okay, I promise. I'm going to make sure of it."

Olivia shifts uncomfortably next to me. Even with all the sexual tension buzzing between us, we still have a job to do. And that's never been more evident than now.

"Enough about all that," Rosita says, strengthening her smile again. "You two go have fun." She wanders away, heading toward her cousin, who I met at last year's Christmas party.

"Are you hungry?" I ask Olivia. The food smells incredible, and Rosita is an amazing cook. I plan on sampling every dish on the table. Maybe twice.

She nods. "Starving, actually, but I'm not sure." Her brow creases as she looks over the colorful dishes of steaming food.

"What's wrong?"

She glances around. "I'm just looking for a knife and fork."

I realize that she's wary of spilling food on her

expensive blouse.

"Come on, I'll help you out. The first time I came here, I bit into a burrito and launched its contents everywhere. It looked like a baby had taken a crap all over my Armani shirt. We couldn't stop laughing."

She looks at me skeptically.

"Rosita taught me the proper way to fold my burrito. There's a trick to it. I'll show you."

She nods and follows me to the table.

We fill our plates with marinated meats, grilled onions, rice, beans, and tortillas. Then we go back for seconds of our favorite dishes. Olivia impresses me with her healthy appetite and adventurous spirit.

After lunch, we mingle and talk with Rosita's family and friends. Even though Olivia says she's enjoying the party—and I believe her—she stays locked by my side all afternoon, attempting polite conversation and smiling nervously. Of all the amazing things she is, "social butterfly" isn't one of them.

I can tell she feels out of place in her six-hundred-dollar sandals, silk blouse, and diamond-encrusted wristwatch. I'm still not sure why she didn't wear something less formal. Or is this the most casual outfit she has in her closet? Maybe she's just incapable of dressing down; she's always manicured from head to toe, the epitome of sophisticated beauty. I certainly won't complain.

She and I didn't grow up like this, with casual backyard parties and paper plates and cans of Sauza beer. The high life definitely has its perks, but given the choice between drinking the best Scotch alone and drinking cheap beer amid friendly laughter, I'll choose this warm sense of family every time.

Later, when the dancing breaks out, I guide Olivia toward the house.

"Now we need some Cuba libres." I head inside, keeping one hand on her lower back to reassure her that I won't leave her to fend for herself.

"Isn't that just rum and Coke?" she asks, skeptical.

"Yes, but it's Mexican Coke, made with real sugar, not that fake corn syrup shit, and the rum . . . Hell, wait until you taste this."

I fill two cups with ice and then the rum-and-Coke mixture Rosita has premixed in a large pitcher.

"Mmm." Olivia moans as she swallows her first fizzy sip.

"Cheers." I gaze down at her and touch the rim of my glass to hers.

"To?" she asks.

"Us," I say, my eyes lingering on hers.

"Noah . . ." She chews on her lower lip. "You know this might not even work, right?" Her tone is somber.

"Like hell it won't. In fact, we really need to get engaged soon."

Maybe it's because I'm feeling jovial and slightly buzzed, but I stand my ground, my eyes still lingering on hers. I've wondered what kind of proposal I'll plan— just a matter-of-fact business meeting where we agree on the terms, or a romantic down-on-one-knee affair where I promise to make this the best I can for her.

Olivia looks down at the floor. "I'm just not ready for that yet."

"I sensed that . . . but you could try." I lean even closer, letting her feel the heat from my body, my height towering over her.

"Try?"

"Yes, *try*."

"And how would you propose I do that?" She's trying her best to sound confident, but her tone has gone shaky.

Feeling bold, I grin at her. "You pulled away last night. You could kiss me, touch me, open up to me, make love to me."

"What, right here?" Her voice rises and her brows pinch together.

"I'd settle for a kiss."

"I've done that before, or have you forgotten?"

"Forgotten? Snowflake, I jack off regularly to the memory."

Her cheeks go bright pink. "Be serious, would you?"

"I am being serious. Does it make you uncomfortable to know that at night, in the dark, I pump my hard cock to thoughts of your sassy attitude, smart mouth, and gorgeous tits?"

Her mouth falls open. Her cheeks are full-on flaming now.

I press on. "One kiss. Hell, you may even end up having fun today." I'm teasing her because I can tell that even though she was tense and awkward when we arrived, she's enjoyed herself today. She just needed a little time to feel at home.

Placing one hand on her waist, I pull her a fraction closer.

Her breathing grows shallow and her lips part, whether in surprise or because she's readying herself for my kiss, I'm not sure.

I lower my mouth to hers, feeling the warmth of her breath ghost over my lips, my cock beginning to swell, when a loud shriek pierces the silence.

"Bee sting. Coming through," Rosita calls, carrying a crying birthday girl through the kitchen.

Stepping away from Olivia, I clear off a space on the counter. "Set her here."

Tears leak from Maria's eyes as quiet sobs rack her chest.

"Shh. I'll make you good as new, princess," I tell Maria.

Olivia and Rosita gather first aid supplies while I distract Maria with a story of the time I wandered into a beehive. Olivia watches me work with a quiet, contemplative gaze, and I can't help but wonder if she would have let me kiss her.

Bringing her here today was no mistake. It goes without saying that people like Rosita and this little girl are one of the main reasons why Olivia and I have to pull this off.

We *have* to.

Chapter Fourteen

Olivia

Dear God, watching Noah with Rosita, and even more so, with little Maria? It was ovary-melting.

I need to keep my cool. Because otherwise? I could easily see myself losing my head over this man.

Chapter Fifteen

Noah

Olivia is always so put together, well dressed in tailored skirts and blouses, manicured from head to toe. It only makes me want to muss her all up and get her dirty. I act like I don't notice her in her business apparel, but of course it affects me. I'm only a man. A man who's apparently taken a vow of celibacy since we began *faux-dating*, or whatever it is we're doing.

God, what are we doing? Any normal Friday night, I'd be out with Sterling chasing tail. Instead I'm sitting at home in sweatpants with a beer and my tablet, doing things I never get to do—like looking up genealogy about my family ancestry and reading random articles on CNN. It's pleasantly relaxing.

But having Olivia here, in my personal space, in our *shared* space all the time is getting distractingly difficult. Like right now, she's perched in a dining chair, legs folded underneath her, a pair of square black-framed glasses balanced on her delicate nose as she stares at her laptop.

It's fucking adorable. She always wears her contacts, and I've rarely seen her like this. It feels good to know that she's comfortable enough to let her guard down with me.

And the fitted Henley that hugs her curves, with its little buttons dotting her chest between her breasts? Don't get me started on those little buttons. I want to undo every last one, bare her to me and nibble my way from one round, perky breast to the other.

"What should we do for dinner, Snowflake?" I call into the dining room where she's busy typing away on her laptop.

"Hmm?" she asks, her gaze taking a moment to drift over to mine.

"It's seven," I tell her.

"Oh, well, don't feel like you have to stay in and cater to me. You can go out or whatever."

She chews on her lip as she says this, though, and something in me knows she'd be out of sorts if I went out without her. Hell, I'd feel the same way. There's a certain peace that comes with working hard with her all week, and now relaxing together.

"I'm in my pajamas. I'm not going out." I chuckle at her.

"Right." She gives me a sly look. "So . . . pizza?"

She normally eats so healthy, and I do too, for that matter, but I like that she doesn't mind cheating and enjoying something just because.

"Hmm, I don't know." I rub my chin. "I think that's the true test of a marriage—can you both agree on the same pizza toppings."

"Okay." She motions for me to go ahead. "You first."

I shake my head. "Same time."

Our gazes lock and she opens her mouth. "Ar—" she starts.

"Artichoke," I say.

She grins at me. "Exactly."

"And maybe sausage?"

She chuckles. "Sure. Why not? Variety is the spice of life."

Maybe that's what marriage is all about—not being the same on every point, but learning to compromise.

I coax her away from her computer when the pizza arrives, waving the warm pie and two bottles of cold beer in front of her.

"Dear God, this is good," she says moments later, moaning around a slice of New York-style pizza.

I nod in agreement. Who knew? Artichokes aren't half bad.

"Here." I hand her a napkin for the smear of sauce on her lower lip.

"Did I get it?" she asks.

"Sure did."

We each enjoy a second slice and the comfortable silence that's settled between us. When we're through, I take the plates into the kitchen and return to the living room. Olivia licks her thumb, leaning back against the couch.

I study her in the way an artist studies his muse. All this time, I keep looking for signs, keep wondering if this could actually work, and while I'm not any closer to an answer, something new has taken shape. I like being near her. I look forward to our time together.

Before I get all fucking mushy, I decide to change the topic to something lighter.

"So . . ." I lean in closer. "This trial period, making out with me, all of it. What are your thoughts so far?"

"Objectively speaking?" she asks, her mouth twitching.

"Of course. I'd like to gauge my performance so far as a fake boyfriend."

"It hasn't been as bad as I would have imagined." Her voice is soft, and she's looking down at her hands.

Camryn's words about Olivia always wanting more—to fall dramatically in love and be swept off her feet—ring loudly in my head. I might not be able to give her everything, but I know I can be a good co-CEO, a good friend, and a good lover. If she'll let me.

Maybe that's not enough, but it's what I have to offer.

"Come here," I murmur, drawing her over onto my lap.

Olivia obeys, straddling my thighs, and places her center right in line with my very interested and semi-erect cock.

I wonder if she's still processing my words from the birthday party—when I asked her to try.

"Closer."

She scoots forward until our lips are inches apart and her warm center is flush with my groin.

I lean in and take her mouth, starting out softly at first so as to not scare my timid princess away. Her lips part for me and I take my time, exploring her mouth with my tongue, sucking on her lips and nibbling lightly.

Olivia's tiny moan of satisfaction makes my pride swell, as well as other things. Growing bold, she circles her hips, and I plant both hands on her waist, urging her to grind down on me. She does—harder this time—and I grunt as my now fully hard shaft is treated to her warm friction.

Tearing my mouth away from hers, I gaze down at her. Those little glasses perched on her nose, her chest flushed and heaving, and those tempting buttons straining over her breasts. She's beautiful like this.

"What is it?" she asks, slightly breathless. "Why'd you stop?"

"I was just thinking. Maybe I can be of service."

She squints her eyes. "Meaning?"

I grip her hips and settle her right over the firm ridge in my pants. "If you'd like to ride this, work out all that frustration from work as you lift and lower yourself on my cock, I'd be game."

"Would you now?" Her tone is light, teasing.

I shrug. "I'd volunteer as tribute."

She laughs, deep and throaty, and it's wonderful.

"And have you win our bet? No way." She shakes her head.

"Okay then, let's call a spade a spade, because we already broke that first-base rule when I had my fingers in your—*delicate flower*—at the restaurant."

"You think my flower is delicate?"

"I do, actually. I think despite that tough-girl act you put on that you're actually sweet and tender and soft on the inside."

Her cheeks grow pink and she looks down.

"You know I wouldn't do anything to hurt you, right?"

She nods without hesitation.

That's good. It means she's beginning to trust me.

Maybe it's a start.

Chapter Sixteen

Olivia

Our whole building buzzes with activity. Even with my office door closed, I can hear the constant low hum of conversation and quick footsteps and ringing phones. I like that white noise; it helps ease me into a productive groove, and it tells me just how many people are working hard alongside me.

Against all odds, we won a small contract from Parrish Footwear—more of a trial period than anything—and also managed to charm back an old client. But will it be enough? We don't have time for any false steps.

And not everyone is making their best effort.

I refresh my in-box and frown. Damn it, Harrison still hasn't sent me that expense summary. I asked him yesterday afternoon, and again when I came in at seven this morning. What the hell has he been doing all this time? That information is at his fingertips; it should have taken him maybe fifteen minutes to round it up.

I consider e-mailing him a third time, then decide against it. The time for nagging has passed. I want him to explain himself in person. Maybe Noah was right about him all along.

I speed-dial the accounting department and ask Harrison's secretary to send him up. And while I wait for him to arrive, I have a very illuminating chat with her about his recent schedule.

He knocks at my door five minutes later. Harrison is in his twenties, and I'm sure many girls find attractive. But to me, he's mostly just unremarkable. The kind of guy people pass on the street every day and don't even remember. Good job. Modest good looks. Average intelligence. None of Noah's wit or charm.

Wait, why am I thinking about Noah?

As Harrison enters, he closes my office door behind him. Can he tell that he's about to get chewed out? Or does he just want privacy to make yet another pass at me?

"Hello, Olivia," he says. "You look beautiful as

always."

I should have known. "Is there some reason why you still haven't completed the work I asked you for yesterday?" I ask him in my frostiest tone.

He blinks. "I . . . had other things on my docket."

"Ahead of a top-priority request from your CEO?"

"Top priority? I didn't know it was that urgent."

I click on my Sent Mail folder, turn my computer screen around to show Harrison our recent e-mail chain, and point at my last sentence.

"Can you read that aloud to me?"

He leans over to squint at the screen. Reluctantly, he recites, "Please send ASAP. I need this report to finish drafting our new budget before the board progress meeting on Thursday."

Then his gaze flicks back to me. "Look, I'm sorry, but I have to fulfill requests in the order they come in. First-come-first-served is the only fair way to—"

"If you can afford to come in late, take two-hour

lunches, and leave early every day, you can afford fifteen minutes to send me a report that I've asked for *twice*." I spin my screen back into position. "Given the company's current crisis, most people at your level of management have been pulling overtime lately. I won't ask you to do that, because I respect my employees' private lives, but if you wish to continue drawing a full-time salary, you will put in full-time hours. Am I making myself clear, Mr. Ridgefield?"

His eyes wide, he licks his lips nervously. "Y-yes, ma'am."

"And the next time you can't finish something with the promptness I need, you should tell me so I can find someone who can. Don't just let my messages sit unanswered in your in-box while I wonder what in the world is going on with your department."

"Yes, ma'am," he repeats. "I will. I'm sorry. You'll get that report by the end of the day."

I nod in acknowledgment. "Thank you. Before lunchtime, if you can." *And if you can't, you'd better have a damn good excuse.*

He turns and starts to walk away. But at the last second, with his hand on the doorknob, he pauses to look back.

I quash a flash of irritation. *Just go do your job and let me do mine.*

"Um, speaking of lunch . . ." He rubs his neck sheepishly, as if some transparent *aw shucks* act will pacify me. "I feel bad about this misunderstanding. Let me take you out today to make up for it."

I level a withering blank stare at him. "This is the fifty-fourth time you've invited me out to eat with you since we met. I've kept count. My answer has always been and will always be no. So instead of trying to distract me from your failures by hitting on me, I suggest you divert some of that energy into your work."

He draws himself up, his hairy nostrils flaring. "Excuse me? Hitting on you? You can't just go around flinging accusations like that. Sexual harassment is a serious—"

"I can do whatever the hell I deem necessary," I snap. "I've tolerated your excuses for long enough. This company is teetering on the edge, and if we want to have any chance of pulling it back, I need to see some serious hustle."

I lock eyes with Harrison, daring him to challenge me. He needs to understand that I'm not just the boss's daughter anymore—let alone some naive intern whose blouse he can peer down while he pretends to help her.

"But if you're not interested in helping me save your job, then by all means, keep testing my patience."

Our staring contest lasts for almost twenty seconds. Finally, his deep brown gaze falters. He looks confused and more than a little pissed, but I think I managed to put the fear of God into him. Then again, only time will tell if he really got the message.

I breathe a sigh of relief as soon as he's gone. My first time bringing down the hammer on an employee went about as well as it could have. But the encounter has still left me irritable and thrown off-kilter.

With my blood pressure already up, I suppress a huff when I see a fresh message in my e-mail in-box. It's Camryn, as the newly minted head of Tate & Cane's newly minted social media team, offering her "top ten picks" for training consultants to hire.

I've never heard of this project. If I had, I would have wanted to be in charge of it. How are they already at the short-list stage? And why is this coming in ahead of the expense estimation that I actually asked for?

Does the universe just not want me to finish this budget today?

Wait a minute . . . maybe I do have an inkling of what this is about. Noah and I revisited the subject of social media training a couple days ago, but I didn't think we actually made a firm decision about anything. That discussion was just brainstorming . . . right? *Evidently he didn't see it that way.*

I call Noah's secretary, only to be reminded that he's out at some executive brunch trying to woo back some more old clients. Too impatient to wait, I call his personal cell instead.

It rings six times before Noah answers dryly, "Yes, dear?" I can hear car engines and rushing wind in the background; he must be on his way back already.

"Since when was Camryn's team researching consultants?" I ask.

"Since we needed to hire some. And since her team is, last time I checked, in charge of social media concerns."

"You know what I mean. Why did you give her the go-ahead on a project that we never finished talking about? Why was this prioritized over my other tasks? And why is she managing it instead of me?"

Noah makes an incredulous noise that sounds way too much like a chortle. "Are you serious? You wanted to be a talent scout?"

"Why not? It's an important decision. Why are you laughing at me?"

He sighs into the phone with a rush of static. "Let me ask you something. Do you think Camryn is an idiot?"

"Of course not." I gasp. "How could you even say that? She's my best friend."

"Because you don't seem to have very much faith

in her competence. For Christ's sake, Olivia, learn to delegate. Your time is so much more valuable than this. Either you or I have to sign off on the final decision anyway, so what's the harm?"

"Dad always taught me that the best way to get something done right is to do it yourself."

Another disbelieving noise, this one more like an outright scoff. "Amazing. You're such a control freak."

"I wouldn't have to be if I could trust people to keep me in the loop!" Somewhere in the back of my mind, I know I'm being irrational, but I've temporarily lost my ability to care.

"Just calm d——" Someone blasts their horn and Noah swears under his breath. "Look, I can't really talk now. I'll be back in ten minutes and we can discuss this."

He hangs up. I drop the phone back in its cradle and massage my forehead. Christ, I don't know how much more disorganization I can take in one day. This clusterfuck is going to give me an ulcer.

After a few minutes of trying to settle down, I give

up and push back my chair. Hopefully a little walk and a change of scenery will help.

I head for the cooler near the front desk and pour myself a cup of ice-cold water. A huge, silvery bubble rises through the tank with a loud *bloop*. Not for the first time, I wonder how dispensing such a small amount of liquid creates such a big bubble.

My time is almost up, and I'm still no closer to knowing for sure if Noah and I will actually work as a married couple. Sure, we've shared some sweet moments, and some smoking-hot ones too.

There were a few of both at Maria's birthday party this weekend. At first, I'd felt like I was intruding on their private family gathering. I hadn't exactly been invited, after all. I was just Noah's girlfriend—and who brings a date to a kid's party, anyway?

But Noah was so reassuring, and everyone welcomed me with open arms. Some of Noah's charisma must have rubbed off on me. Although I could have done without Rosita's little congratulatory winks.

Once again, I was reminded of a mother doting proudly on her son. Noah was definitely part of her family. He made a point of catching up with everyone at the party, not just the general "how's work?" kind of icebreaker, but specific questions like "Is your cousin out of his leg cast yet?" or "Did you get that promotion you were planning to ask for?" He obviously tries hard to remember the details of their lives.

But maybe that isn't so surprising. Even though Noah can be self-absorbed sometimes, he's a real people person. That gift of gab sometimes makes me jealous . . . when it doesn't sweep me off my feet like everyone else he interacts with. He's always so comfortable in his own skin, so at home in any situation. He looked just as natural in shorts and a silly paper hat, roughhousing with kids in a muddy backyard, as he does in a three-piece bespoke suit at an executive luncheon.

Watching him laugh that day . . . it's definitely persuaded me to let him get closer.

Okay, so Noah is a decent man. A pretty great one, even. But does that mean I have to let go of my dream of falling madly in love someday?

What I need is a sign.

I let my gaze drift across the reception area as I drink my water. The front door swings open, and for a second, I think Noah must have made it back in record time.

Then I recognize the man and I almost choke. *Oh no. No, no, no . . .*

My stomach clenches as every nerve lights up with a fight-or-flight impulse. I can't even tell if I'm terrified or furious—this feeling is just raw, undifferentiated adrenaline.

It's Bradford Daniels, my ex-boyfriend from hell, standing just a few yards away. What the fuck is he doing here? I thought I was done with him forever. I thought I'd escaped. But now he's in my building, my sanctuary, and I had no warning at all and *I'm not ready.*

Stunned, my heart hammering in my chest, I watch him like a deer in the headlights as he checks in at the front desk. He leans close to the receptionist. I can't hear what he says, but I can guess by his flirtatious smile and her answering giggle.

It's not her fault. Brad's handsome face and country-club manners once tricked me too. She can't know any better. Can't see the slimy soul hiding underneath.

I started dating Brad in college because he was hot, he came from a prestigious family, and he was the first guy I've ever met who shared my hard-driving ambition. But I discovered too late that his competitive spirit was untempered by any sense of fair play. All the privilege he was born into, as staggering as it was, still didn't satisfy him. He felt entitled to more—by any means necessary.

His father was the only person he felt true loyalty to. Everyone else in the world existed to use for his own benefit. And what made him really dangerous was his ability to disguise his predatory selfishness. He blatantly used his inferiors because he knew he could get away with it, but he sucked up to his superiors and manipulated his peers so skillfully that nobody with any power to stop him ever caught on to his games.

I still hate to admit just how long I let Brad use me. He had me convinced that he was trying his best to love me and I was the one being "difficult." I clung to the scraps of affection he rationed out when and only when he wanted something from me.

It took me over two years to realize that Brad—not my "difficult" personality, not the stress from my classes and internships and club duties—was the reason I was so miserable all the time. It took another six months for me to do something about that revelation. I broke up with him at our graduation ceremony so I'd never have to see him again.

Or so I thought.

Brad turns and spots me. Noticing my appalled stare, he gives me a sarcastic little wave.

Rage wins out over panic. My paralysis shatters. After spiking my paper cup into the trash can, I charge over to him like a mother wolf defending my den.

"Get out," I growl.

The receptionist blinks, startled by my unbridled hatred.

Brad, of course, doesn't look at all surprised. He

knows exactly how I feel about him—and why. But he'll never pass up an opportunity to make me look like a crazy bitch.

"What, not even a hello?" he asks, feigning hurt.

Too bad I don't care how I look. Everyone in this building is loyal to my family; I can afford to deal with Brad first and explain myself later.

"You don't deserve one. Leave now."

He looks down his nose with a condescending smile. "Oversensitive as always . . . how unprofessional. I have a right to be here. My father's in the market to acquire a new subsidiary, so I'm here to pay your board a visit."

"This company still belongs to the Tate and Cane families. You can't buy a single brick in our building yet, and until that day comes, you're just snooping around. Wait your turn like everybody else." It's bad enough that WBB was allowed in . . . and I don't have a gory personal history with them.

His sneer deepens into overt disdain. "You can't treat me like this. I was invited here."

"And I have the power to un-invite you. So you can slink right back to your corner office and crawl into Daddy's lap like you always do."

Brad's eyes narrow to dangerous slits. He snarls, "You dried-up bitch—!"

I scoff audibly. If I ever was dried up, whose fault does Brad think that was? He should have looked up *foreplay* in a dictionary sometime.

With a twinge of childish satisfaction, I note that the receptionist is now staring in shock at Brad instead of me. Then I'm filled with shame at my pettiness. *This is what Brad reduces me to. One minute in his presence, and I've stooped to his level.* As if the years since our breakup never happened.

At my derisive noise, Brad pulls his features back into haughty coolness, under the cover of straightening his tie. I remember—all too well—his insecure need to maintain control at all times, even if it's only the appearance of control.

"You might want to be a lot more careful about how you speak to me, Olivia."

The obvious threat spooks me a little. But I can't let him know how much his venomous voice still affects me. I force a laugh, knowing that will drive him ape-shit.

"Or what? You'll bore me to death?"

To my surprise, his smirk doesn't slip an inch. "Trust me. It's in your best interests to cooperate with my company."

Does he actually have something up his sleeve? On the one hand, I don't want to get drawn into his mind games. On the other . . . my curiosity is piqued.

But before I can decide whether to venture a question, the front door opens and Noah comes in. He stops midstride, looking back and forth between us, obviously sensing something rotten in the air.

"What's going on here?" he demands.

"Nothing," Brad replies before I can explain anything, his tone light and his smile polite. "Just talking shop."

"Oh, really? Is that why I could hear a man yelling all the way from the elevator?"

Brad's smile instantly drops. "Who are you?" he asks, as if Noah were the one intruding.

"I'm Noah Tate. Olivia's fiancé and co-CEO. Now, who the hell are you?"

I mentally roll my eyes a little at Noah's lack of subtlety. Especially the way he said *fiancé* instead of *boyfriend*. But mostly, I'm just relieved to have some backup, no matter how silly his testosterone-fueled territorial display is.

Brad stares Noah down for a moment, obviously not wanting to roll over and acknowledge his authority too fast. Finally, he replies, "Bradford Daniels. Vice president of Daniels Multimedia Enterprises."

"And he was just leaving," I interrupt.

I see a muscle twitch in Brad's jaw, but he continues talking to Noah as if I never said a word.

"I've heard of you, Noah. The late Bill Tate's son. You two seem to have hooked up right before news of Tate & Cane's . . . difficulties got out."

Noah's next words echo my thoughts. "Are you

implying something?"

"Not at all. Just commenting on a stroke of bad luck." Brad drops his voice to a conspiratorial mutter—although it's certainly not low enough to stop me from hearing every insult. "In more ways than one. Between you and me, my friend, I don't envy you. She's about as exciting as a wet towel in bed."

Noah's eyes fly open wide and his face flushes crimson. Instinctively I shy back; I've never seen him so angry.

Mistaking his fury for astonishment, Brad continues. "Oh, you haven't found that out yet? But maybe I shouldn't be surprised. She's always been such a frigid—"

In a flash, Noah has Brad pinned to the wall, his arm twisted behind his back. And all I can do is gape, paralyzed with shock.

Chapter Seventeen

Noah

This is the douche who broke Olivia's heart in college? Without thinking, I jump into action, twisting the prick's arm behind his back and slamming him into the wall.

He lets out a helpless grunt and huffs, "What the hell? Did you not hear who I am?"

"I know exactly who you are. You're the pencil-dick Olivia invested years in, only to discover what a selfish child you really are."

He tugs against the hold I have on him. *Nope, you're not going anywhere, bud.*

"Now apologize to her, with a promise that you'll never say anything like that again, and I'll think about letting you go."

"Like hell," he growls.

"Rosita," I call out. She's passing by with her cart

filled with deliveries. "Call security." She nods once and scurries away. I twist Bradford's arm tighter, higher up behind his back, then lean in good and close. "I said apologize."

He blows out a deep sigh, his voice taut with pain. "I'm sorry, all right?"

When Olivia turns up her nose, I shake my head at the poor schmuck. "You should know better than to fuck with such a powerful woman."

Two uniformed security guards appear in an instant. "Remove this asshole from the property," I tell them.

They flank Bradford and escort him back to the elevator. I brace myself for another insult hurled over his shoulder; there's no way he's going down without a fight.

Right on cue, Bradford turns to face us before entering the elevator. "When I own this company, I'll be the one calling the shots, and neither of you will ever work in this town again," he shouts, spitting the words like venom.

I straighten my posture and pull Olivia in close to my side. "You won't be coming into my building and insulting *my girl* like that ever again. Get him out of here before I permanently remove his option of ever having children."

Moments later, the elevator doors slide closed, and Olivia sags against my side in relief.

"Are you okay?" I turn to face her, running my hands in a soothing motion up and down her arms.

She nods once, her lips pulled into a tight line.

I lean down and press my lips to hers, needing to erase that pout.

"He's gone, baby," I murmur, stroking her hair.

She takes a deep breath and lets it out slowly. "He's such a massive A-hole," she mutters, shaking her head. "What did I ever see in him?"

Her tone drips angry contempt but I can hear the quiver underneath. Brad must have really rattled her. I clench my teeth. Maybe I shouldn't have let that fucker get away unscathed after all.

"I won't let him come near you again. That's a promise."

She nods. "Thank you, Noah."

We're both quiet for a moment, as if neither of us is quite ready to part ways and get back to work. Olivia gazes up at me with relief, gratitude . . . and something more? There's a new light in her eyes. A look she's never given me before.

"Not that I need you to defend my honor, but . . ." She gives me a small smile. "I'm glad you did."

Pride and protectiveness swell in my chest. I try to brush it off by joking. "Hey, no problem. His face was begging for a punch anyway."

She pats me on the chest, and I turn to head down the hall toward my office.

"Noah?"

That one word stops me in my tracks. Her voice is soft, almost shy, yet brimming with emotion. I've never heard Olivia talk so . . . I don't know the word. Tenderly? Whatever it is, it floats me up like a boat on a rising tide.

"Yes?" I turn to face her.

Her face is awash in enlightenment as if she's just been struck by a thought. "I think I'm ready."

Did I hear her right? I almost don't dare to hope. "You mean . . . ?"

She nods, biting back the first hint of a grin.

My heart surges. "Then let's fucking do this."

She beams at me as if we're both on the inside of a private joke. And maybe we are.

"Let's freaking get married," she says with a giggle.

Chapter Eighteen

Olivia

I squint at the clock on my nightstand and suppress a groan. Three in the goddamn morning and I'm still wide awake.

The sheets rustle behind me. "Can't sleep?" Noah asks. His voice is clear, not groggy at all. Evidently I'm not the only one with insomnia.

Sighing, I shake my head.

"Come here," he says gently.

I roll over to look at him. Noah is lying on his side, facing me. He holds out his top arm. I hesitate for a moment; I'm still getting used to casual contact with him. But soon I wriggle into his warm embrace, pillowing my head on his bicep.

He pulls me even closer with an arm around my shoulders. I inhale his masculine scent, no less pleasant and exciting for how familiar it's become, and try not to notice how perfectly I fit nestled in against his side.

"How do you feel?" he asks.

"A little nervous," I confess.

Noah gives a quiet hum of a chuckle. "I wouldn't blame you. It's normal to have a few pre-wedding jitters."

The word *wedding* sits oddly in my stomach. Despite all the thought I've put into the idea of marriage over the past month, it feels totally different when it's on the horizon. In less than sixteen hours, I won't be single anymore. I'll be someone's wife.

I've always imagined myself getting married someday. But in that fantasy, my father would walk me down a wide church aisle, the pews decorated with peonies, as my elated friends and extended family looked on. My husband would be a man who loved me so deeply that he couldn't stand to live a single day without me.

But the reality of my life is nothing like that sweet story. Instead, I bear the pressure of a legally binding contract, followed by a long, hard battle to keep Tate &

Cane out of enemy hands.

The circumstances definitely leave a lot to be desired. My feelings about the groom himself, though . . . those are way more ambiguous.

Things between us used to be simple. Noah was just a plain old pain in my ass. An acquaintance at best; a rival or a pest at worst. His devil-may-care attitude still infuriates me sometimes. And I hate the way he knows exactly how handsome he is, and shamelessly uses his good looks to get what he wants. Although what I really hate may be the fact that his charm works on me too, whether I like it or not. No matter how hard I try, I've never been able to completely bury my huge crush on him.

Lately, though, everything is changing. We're well on the road to becoming friends now. And seeing him leap to my defense against Brad gave me undeniable butterflies.

Noah has lived up to my challenge and convinced me that a relationship between us is possible. Not right away, and not without effort—this isn't a fairy tale where we snap our fingers and live happily ever after—

but if we keep trying in good faith . . .

I'm even starting to wonder if my feelings for him when I was a teenager weren't totally unfounded. Maybe my younger self was on to something. Maybe she wasn't just horny—okay, horniness was definitely a factor, but still. She sensed a passionate, fiercely kind heart beating underneath his playboy facade. I've learned that just because Noah doesn't take everything seriously doesn't mean he doesn't take *anything* seriously. His priorities and strategies are different from mine, not necessarily better or worse.

A dozen different emotions swirl through me, some good, some bad. But even though Noah asked me, I'm reluctant to reveal them all. Because I don't want to show vulnerability . . . or because I don't want to hurt his feelings? I'm not sure.

Eventually, unable to decide how to reply, I just murmur into his chest, "It's still kind of surreal to me, you know?"

"Yeah." Noah gives me a reassuring squeeze . . . and presses his lips to my forehead.

I blink at his feather-soft kiss. The unexpected tenderness just muddles my feelings more.

Oblivious to my confusion, Noah lies on his back, drawing my arm around his waist. I try to push my distracting, troubling thoughts away and relax into him. I cuddle closer, pushing my head onto his chest and resting my leg over his. He's so warm, like lying next to a fireplace.

The steady beat of his heart beneath my ear soothes me to sleep.

Chapter Nineteen

Noah

As far as the media's concerned, a couple of our status should have a wedding with glitz and swagger, but Olivia decided she felt most comfortable having our ceremony at her father's beach house on Nantucket. It's a purely legal wedding. No fanfare, just a handful of family and close friends. Even the beach house itself is a quaint place, with just two bedrooms, an open-plan kitchen and living space, and a wide porch looking out onto the beach.

That stretch of beach is where we'll tie the proverbial knot in about an hour. Drinking beer in the kitchen with Sterling, I watch seagulls land on the folding chairs we set up earlier, scaring a few tiny crabs back into their holes.

This whole affair is the polar opposite of what Camryn told me about Olivia's scrapbook wedding. And I don't know how to feel about that. Did Olivia just want to keep things convenient and cheap? She is the practical type, and she's been tearing her hair out over Tate & Cane's expenses recently.

Or is she trying to preserve her romantic dream by keeping her reality as far away from it as possible? I'm not sure I like that idea, considering I'm part of her reality . . .

"Another beer?" Sterling asks.

"I better not." I glance at the clock hanging on the kitchen wall. "Fifty-eight minutes till I say I do."

My best man smirks. "You think she's actually going to go through with it?"

"You don't?"

He shrugs. "She locked herself in her room two hours ago and hasn't been out since. I offered her breakfast this morning, and she said she was too uneasy to eat. I don't know, man. It's entirely possible that she'll back out."

"The contract's all drawn up. We'll sign it on Monday when we're back at the office. Why back out now? Olivia's a woman of her word. She's dependable like that."

He lets out a grunt of disapproval.

"What's the big deal? You took a fake date to prom," I remind him.

I chuckle to myself, remembering the year Sterling took his cousin to the dance. He thought it was genius at the time—no corsage to buy, no need to impress her with a fancy restaurant or limo ride. Until the end of the night, when all the rest of us were enjoying some skin-to-skin contact with our dates, and he realized what a horrible decision he'd made. The only skin-to-skin action he got was with his hand.

"A fake wife is a hell of a lot different. It's a big fucking deal." Sterling glares at me over the rim of his beer.

Looking out over the ocean from our spot on the porch of the beach cottage, I loosen my tie, which has grown too tight around my neck, and level him with a dark stare.

"Actually, it's legally binding, so she'll be my real wife. Until we got divorced, or got the marriage annulled or whatever."

I clear my throat, my unease growing. "Oh, one more thing."

After Olivia's father presented the contract to us this morning over breakfast, I took a copy with me out to the porch while Olivia retreated to the bedroom. I didn't view it as a bad sign, just that we were both taking this seriously and needed a moment to absorb it.

With a cup of coffee, I read the contract in full detail. Page fourteen, section twenty-eight, part B stated that the fulfillment of our contractual obligations as new owners of the multi-billion-dollar conglomerate was also contingent on Olivia getting pregnant. Within ninety days.

I stormed inside to talk to Fred immediately.

"An heir clause? Is this your sick way of ensuring the family name carries on? You actually expect me to knock her up?"

"It's part of your father's will, Noah. Bill and I both wanted a grandchild before we died. Surely you can understand that."

"And what has Olivia said about that?" I asked him.

He made a noncommittal noise in his throat. "We haven't discussed it yet."

That was this morning. And I'm pretty sure that's the reason Olivia locked herself inside her bedroom and hasn't been seen since.

Taking a deep sigh, I watch my best man carefully as I drop my news. "I need to knock her up."

Sterling spits out his drink.

"There's an heir clause in the contract," I say dryly.

Wiping beer from his lips, he narrows his eyes on mine. "You're telling me you need to impregnate her?"

"Uh-huh."

The fucker actually laughs at me, then takes another sip of his beer. "If I know the first thing about Olivia, it's that she's not going to want your bun in her oven."

"O, ye of little faith." I smirk at him.

"Has she even touched your cock yet?"

Aside from grabbing it through my slacks once at the restaurant, no. But that doesn't mean anything. We're building on something good here. It's only a matter of time.

"Don't be an ass."

I stand up and cross the porch to the railing, leaning on it as I look out on the endless pool of blue lapping at the shoreline. I may be putting on a cool and unaffected front about all of this, but in fact, I've been losing my shit ever since I learned about the clause in the contract this morning. I can only imagine how Olivia feels. I don't even know if she wants to be a mother. Probably not, seeing as she eats, sleeps, and breathes her career.

"You're good, buddy, I'll give you that, but even *you* won't be able to pull this one off."

"We'll see about that."

Watching the water is hypnotic. It makes me feel slightly calmer. But only slightly. I'd probably need horse tranquilizers to get anywhere close to a normal heart rate.

"And what about you? The reigning party animal is seriously going to have a baby?"

I turn back to face Sterling. He's kicked back in a weather-beaten rocker on the porch, one leg hooked over the arm of it. With no good answer for him, I just give him a cocky wink.

"I'll figure it out." *I hope.*

His mouth drops open for a second. Then he throws up his hands in a dramatic shrug. "It's your life, man."

"I'll take my chances. Now, if you'll excuse me, I'm going to check on my bride."

I knock on the closed door of the bedroom Olivia set up in and hear the two feminine voices inside hush.

"Yes?" Camryn opens the door just a crack.

"Can I have a minute with Olivia?" I ask.

Camryn's brow furrows. "It's bad luck to see the bride before the ceremony."

"It's okay," Olivia says from inside.

"Fine. You can talk with her for five minutes." Camryn glancing at her watch and then skirts around me into the hall.

When I push open the door, I find Olivia seated at a vanity, and our reflections meet in the mirror. Her eyes are rimmed in red, and I wonder if she's been crying.

Guilt stabs at my chest and I suddenly feel short of breath. "Are you okay?"

I can't believe how much my relationship with Olivia has grown, how real my feelings have become. The thought of her so upset feels like a physical shove.

She nods. "I think so. Today's been strangely emotional. All these things I haven't thought about in a while, like my mom not being here, my dad's health . . . it all hit me this morning."

"Come here."

I pull her to her feet and into my arms. As I bring her close to my chest, her hands settle on my back. I hold her for several minutes, neither of us speaking. When I let her go, Olivia looks more composed. I wonder how she feels about the heir clause—wonder if she's on board, indifferent, or terrified. I'm guessing the latter.

"I'm okay. I promise." She gives me a small smile.

"You look beautiful," I tell her, meaning every word.

She looks down at her simple cream-colored sundress with lace trimming the bust, and smooths it over her hips. "Thank you." Her honey-colored hair flows in loose waves over her shoulders, and her makeup is light and natural. She looks like the perfect casual beach bride, fit to grace the cover of one of those bridal magazines.

"Are you sure you aren't going to regret this?" I ask, the moment taking a turn for the serious. I probably won't love her answer, but I still want to know her honest feelings.

She shakes her head. "All I've ever wanted is to run this company. My dad's been grooming me for this moment for fifteen years."

I nod, understanding perfectly. We're in the same position.

"And if I have to do it with you by my side, so be it."

Olivia thrusts her chin up in the air, and I'm again struck by guilt. She's putting on a brave front, but I need to know she's okay. Otherwise, I'm not sure I can go through with this.

"I need to know if you're really okay doing things this way. Doesn't every girl dream about a white dress and a big party under a tent?" I know for a fact that Olivia does. But I don't mention that; she may not have wanted Camryn to tell me something so personal.

She gives me a sympathetic look. "We'll make it work."

"It might not be the wedding you envisioned, but I want you to know that it is to me. I really would take care of you if anything bad happened. I know what we have isn't love, and that you deserve to be loved and cherished by your husband, but I need you to know I'll always step up and be there for you. So in that sense, my vows will all be true."

She swallows, and I wonder if there's a lump stuck in her throat like there is in mine. That thought eases some of my guilt the smallest bit.

"Thank you for that. I know you'll be there for me when it matters," she says, her tone soft.

"Damn straight, I will."

"Thanks, Noah." She smiles at me.

I pull the creased contract from the inside pocket of my jacket. "I went ahead and signed this. So, whenever you're ready." I hand her the contract, and she sets it down on her vanity table.

"Thank you."

I lift her hand to my mouth and kiss it. "See you out there."

She nods. "I'll just be a few more minutes."

"Okay. I'll send Camryn back in."

As I head out into the hall, I'm struck by the

feeling that maybe, just maybe, Sterling is wrong, and all of this will unfold naturally between me and Olivia.

Call me crazy, but hell, it may just work.

Chapter Twenty

Olivia

I'm at my family's summer cottage on Nantucket Island, motionless while Camryn puts the finishing touches on my eye makeup. This bedroom is still decorated according to my tastes in my high school days—which apparently involved a lot of tie-dye, mandala posters, and framed rain forest photos. Heh . . . I'd forgotten I had a hippie phase. At its small whitewashed desk, where I sit now, I did my summer homework and wrote in my diary.

Thank God for Camryn. She drove over early to lend a hand before the ceremony. As far as primping goes, I didn't really need her help. I'm not doing anything special with my hair or makeup. My only concession to the special occasion is a cream-colored dress, and even that is pretty plain: just a knee-length wrap with a little lace at the bust. I look more like the mother of a bride than the bride herself. What I did need—desperately—was my best friend's moral support. Her calm, matter-of-fact presence soothes my frazzled nerves.

I don't even know why I'm wound so tight. Our "wedding" is just Noah and me meeting with a justice of the peace to sign the paperwork, while Dad and a few other family members and close friends stand by. No tuxedo and gown, no vows, no reception party. As short and simple as humanly possible. This marriage isn't even real . . . and yet I have a textbook case of cold feet.

"And boom," Camryn announces proudly. "Eyes are all done. Take a look."

I open my eyes and blink at myself in the mirror. Wow, I look . . . hot. My usual makeup style is pretty minimalistic, since I rarely go anywhere besides the office, but Camryn has given me a subtle smokiness that's sensual while still being demure enough for a daytime event.

"This looks great. Thank you."

"Am I good or what?" Camryn grins. "Do you want anything to eat? Now's your last chance before I do your lips."

The kitchen counters and breakfast bar are piled with casseroles and salads and finger sandwiches from the catering company Dad hired. I told him I didn't want a reception with a fancy meal afterward. But he insisted that our guests, as few as they are, still need to eat before heading back home. So this was our compromise, self-serve casual fare on paper plates.

I shake my head. "No, thanks. My stomach is flip-flopping like crazy."

"That bad?" Camryn asks, her tone rising in sympathy.

I let out a deep sigh. "Honestly? I'm not sure how I feel."

I really do believe that Noah and I can work as a couple. But I'm still on the verge of panic. Marriage is such a huge commitment. Thinking about taking that step—oh God, and in less than an hour too—makes me break out in a cold sweat.

If Camryn hadn't been here to steady my nerves, I might have seriously considered bolting. Especially when Dad handed over a copy of the contract at breakfast—all looming and official with its sixteen numbered pages. I still haven't been able to bring myself to look at it. But I already know what it says, anyway. What's the point of stressing myself out even more? I'll just sign it when the time comes, quick and easy, like ripping off a bandage.

"Poor thing." Camryn sighs. "Let me get you a drink. You need a little something to take the edge off."

She bustles out of the bedroom to visit the kitchen and comes back with two glasses of merlot. My best friend knows me well enough to forgo the bottle of chilled champagne nestled in its ice bucket on the kitchen counter. Champagne is much too celebratory for the mood I'm in.

I accept the pleasantly chilled glass and take a deep swig. The small dose of alcohol subtly warms and loosens my muscles, and I let out a quiet sigh. She was right; I did need this.

"I really think this will be okay," Camryn says. "From what I've seen, it seems like Noah's been pretty sweet and attentive toward you."

"Yeah, I do think he's really trying." I take another sip of my wine. "Even if his ultimate goal is just to get into my pants."

"And that would be the worst thing in the world, why?" She raises her eyebrows at me with a devilish grin. She's continuously griping about the state of my nonexistent love life.

I snort, smiling back despite myself. "I have about as much interest in riding his knob as I do in jumping off the Brooklyn Bridge."

Except when the jerk does something sexy and all the blood in my brain suddenly flies south for the winter. Which seems to be happening more and more often lately.

"Ladies ..." Sterling pokes his head around the door frame, smirking like he heard every word. "Knob riding will commence after dinner." Then he tips his chin toward us and leaves.

Fuck. The last thing I need is Noah thinking that tonight will feature any wedding-night hanky-panky. Frustrated, I growl and slam my eyes closed.

"We need something stronger than wine." Camryn charges back into the kitchen before I can stop her. I can hear clattering as she searches through cabinets. Soon she returns, holding out a bottle of vodka. "Here we go."

"No, that's okay." I wave her off. "I don't really want to get too tipsy right now."

She sets down the vodka on the desk. "Good point. We should wait until after the ceremony."

"Actually . . ." I sigh. "I'm sorry, I don't think I'll be in the mood to socialize tonight. I need some time alone to figure stuff out." Or bury my head in work like an ostrich and avoid my situation entirely. "Thank you for coming all the way out here."

She nods. "Of course I came, Olivia. I can head back to the city early, no problem. It's a long trip back anyway." Her gaze wanders over toward the deck where Noah and Sterling sit with their backs to us, looking out over the beach. "Then again, Sterling's pretty fucking hot. I could probably busy myself with him tonight." She grins wickedly.

"Knock yourself out," I say with a shrug. Someone around here should have fun, after all. "In fact, go ahead and get him now. I can do my lipstick by myself."

We share one last reassuring hug before she leaves me alone in my childhood bedroom, taking her drink with her.

I push up the window and inhale the saltiness of the humid ocean breeze. The afternoon is warm, and mist rises from the blue harbor. For a minute, I watch a handful of distant sailboats, dim white dots bobbing on the horizon. I try not to obsess about the ceremony that will be starting in just half an hour. Letting the peaceful view fill my mind, I feel my tension start to melt away.

But the blessed silence shatters when my phone rings. Grumbling, wondering who the hell would call me right now, I dig it out of my purse.

I frown at the screen. Since I don't know this number off the top of my head, I answer with a brisk, "Hello?"

"Good afternoon, Olivia."

My stomach contracts into a tight, painful ball. *That*

voice . . . For a moment I can't speak.

"You really should check your e-mail more often," Brad says.

Chapter Twenty-One

Noah

I've been standing on the beach for fifty minutes. Beads of sweat dot my forehead, but they're not from the sun. That set ten minutes ago.

"Where is she?" Sterling hisses under his breath.

"She'll be here," I say through gritted teeth, checking my watch yet again.

After everything we've built . . . living together, working together . . . it all feels so fragile and pointless if Olivia doesn't follow through today.

Guests are starting to look at each other, and hushed whispers rustle through the small crowd.

The officiant shifts her weight, looking as uncomfortable as I feel. Then she leans in toward me. "I'm terribly sorry, but I have an appointment in twenty minutes. I can't wait much longer."

I nod and look to Fred. His features are twisted

with worry. When he tips his chin toward Camryn, she scurries off toward the house. I take off after her, stepping into the footprints she leaves in the sand.

We head straight for the bedroom. The house is dim, and the feeling that something fundamental has changed rips through me. The door is still shut, and I'm afraid of what we'll find when she opens it. Afraid of what it will mean.

Finally, Camryn opens the door. Everything is quiet for a minute.

"She's gone," she says, her voice shaky.

I swallow down a wave of emotion and look around the room. Olivia's makeup and toiletries are still scattered on the vanity, but she's not in the room.

I stare out the window at the sun setting over the ocean, and let out a heavy sigh. "She's gone."

What in the hell could possibly happened since I last saw her? She was ready. Everything seemed fine. I notice the contract is no longer sitting on the vanity table. She's taken it with her. I'm not sure what that means.

I turn to face Camryn. "What happened? You were the last person to see her. Was it nerves?"

Camryn shakes her head. "She seemed fine."

I push my hands into my hair. I don't fucking like surprises, and I've never been stood up before. But getting left at the altar? This is beyond any anger and panic I've ever felt.

I want to go out drinking and find some random girl so I can fuck out my aggression. And I know Sterling would be game. But then I think of Olivia's shy smile and her sweet honeysuckle scent and the way her lips part when I kiss her . . . silently begging me for more.

"Fuck this," Sterling says from behind me. "We're leaving. Come on, Noah."

His hand closes around my arm and starts tugging me down the hall. I know he has the exact same thought I did about thirty seconds ago. Booze. Girls. Massive hangover tomorrow to mask the pain of today. But I know nothing could blot out this memory.

If it weren't for this ache in my chest—this empty

spot she'd begun to fill—I'd leave and never look back. But part of me needs to know the next chapter in our story.

I've fantasized about Olivia for the last twenty years. She's the girl I squirted with the water hose when I was young, the woman who gave me butterflies in my stomach when I was older.

And now, just as I've started to think of her as mine . . . she's gone.

Coming Soon

Hitched, Volume Two

I did it. I mustered up the courage and handed my new fake husband a signed contract.

I've made up my mind. Even if my new husband is cocky and arrogant, he's like candy for my libido. Sweet, sugary candy. I know he's bad for me, but I want to devour every inch of him.

With his sexual prowess and experience, something tells me he'll be explosive in the bedroom. I can only imagine the tricks up his sleeve—or rather, in his pants. And since we're stuck together for the foreseeable future, keeping this marriage charade up long enough to turn the company profitable again—which will be no small feat—I deserve something to look forward to at the end of a long workday.

I'm a mature, responsible woman. I'm going to begin fucking my husband.

There, I said it. I'm going to enjoy some marital

sex. I just need him to understand this is about fucking. Nothing more.

Acknowledgments

I would like to thank the following ladies who played an important role in helping me bring *Hitched* into the world: Alexandra Fresch, Hang Le, Natasha Gentile, Rachel Brookes, Danielle Sanchez, and Pam Berehulke. I'm so grateful to have each of you on my team.

A big thank you to Crystal Patriarche and the BookSparks Team.

And to John. Always John.

About the Author

A *New York Times*, *Wall Street Journal*, and *USA TODAY* bestselling author of more than twenty titles, Kendall Ryan has sold more than 1.5 million e-books, and her books have been translated into several languages in countries around the world. She's a traditionally published author with Simon & Schuster and Harper Collins UK, as well as an independently published author.

Since she first began self-publishing in 2012, she's appeared at #1 on Barnes & Noble and iBooks charts around the world. Her books have also appeared on the *New York Times* and *USA TODAY* bestseller list more than two dozen times. Ryan has been featured in such publications as *USA TODAY*, *Newsweek*, and *In Touch Weekly*.

Visit Kendall at: www.kendallryanbooks.com

Other Books by Kendall Ryan

Unravel Me

Make Me Yours

Working It

Craving Him

All or Nothing

When I Break

When I Surrender

When We Fall

Filthy Beautiful Lies

Filthy Beautiful Love

Filthy Beautiful Lust

Filthy Beautiful Forever

The Gentleman Mentor

Sinfully Mine

Bait & Switch

Slow & Steady

Hard to Love

Reckless Love

Resisting Her